THE WRONG
SHADOW

FOX RIVER HAUNTINGS

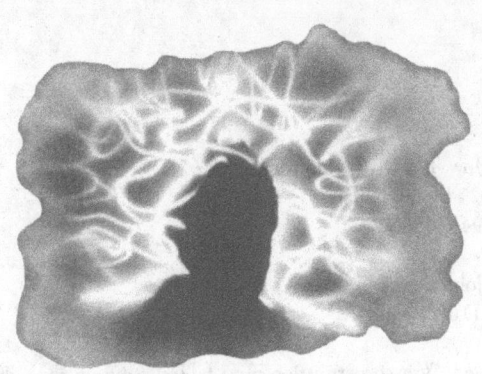

BILL GILLARD

The Wrong Shadow: Fox River Hauntings
Copyright © 2025 by Bill Gillard
SC ISBN: 9781948365666

Cover photo by John Beaver
Cover design by Dana Breunig

Published by Ten16 Press, an imprint of Orange Hat Publishing

www.orangehatpublishing.com
Wauwatosa, WI

This book is a work of fiction. Names, characters, places and incidents are the product of the author's imagination or are used fictitiously.

CONTENTS

CONTENTS

BURYING
THE DEAD

Henry came back home to Menasha on a cold, rainy, early Sunday morning in April 1953. The sky had only just started to brighten. As the Greyhound roared away in a cloud of exhaust, he slung his duffle bag over his shoulder and turned up the collar on his pea coat. Felt strange to be home, especially so soon after leaving for the war. Got the letter about his parents and the Army discharged him and shipped him out two days later. Now he was back home in Wisconsin, his mind whirling, away from the sticky, hot jungle of Korea, away from the war-wounded, the choppers, the snipers at night, always on the move. Back home to America, land of all-night burger drive-ins, hot rod cars, sock hops, big band swing, and happy, safe people. A world away, his buddies joked about the day they'd return, the unprintable things they'd do when they got alone with their sweethearts. It passed the time, thinking about home.

Henry made it home before any of the others did. He didn't even need to get shot or blown up or broken. His parents had taken the hit instead. Like they were saving him again, like they always said they would. He stood at the corner of Main and looked up Racine Street toward the house he grew up in. He remembered the last time he walked to this bus stop. Mom and Dad were with him. Dad slapped him on the back, said he was proud of his boy, but Henry could see in his eyes the fear, the doubt, as he helped his only son load a suitcase onto the bus. And Henry's mom, tears in her eyes, dug her fingernails into his arms until he pulled away from her, smoothing his immaculately clean and pressed shirt. "Mom, you're embarrassing me..." But now he wished he had let her hold on with all her might, never let him go so far away to see the death and killing he saw over there. And the last thing she told him? Henry could never forget that. "If they'd take me, I'd go in your place. I promise you I would." She said it so calmly, but with a wild look in her eye.

Henry trudged north on Racine, afraid of what awaited him. It had been four weeks already, but he dreamed again and again that he would arrive home, and the fire would still be raging and his parents would still be in the upper windows screaming for help. In his dreams, the blistering heat would not let him get close enough. The fire always won.

Only half a block now, and the neighborhood slept. No sign of fire engine, police, or red glow. He knew every line in the pavement, every curbstone. All of it. And the little white house with the big elm in the front yard.

Five more houses.

Four.

Two.

Henry stood in the middle of the silent road, rain pelting him, drops trickling under his shirt and down his back.

Where his house had been was now a mess. A dumpster filled with charred wood scraps rested next to the open foundation. The brick chimney stood, but only to about half its original height.

He walked silently across the front yard to where the front door had been. He investigated the gaping hole. Small piles of twisted, blackened wood, pipes, wires, and half-burnt hunks of furniture were piled in mounds on the floor of the cellar.

As he made his way halfway around the world, from Seoul to Honolulu to San Francisco to Chicago to Menasha, he received four telegrams, one every couple of days, from the city of Menasha.

The first told him the city wanted the place cleaned up.

The second told him they couldn't wait any longer for him to come home.

Third, if they found anything worth saving, they'd keep it for him.

The last one said they found nothing worth keeping—all was to be disposed of as soon as the sanitation men could get to it.

Henry dropped his duffle bag into the open foundation and climbed gingerly down into the hole. He kicked at the burnt remains of a dining room chair and climbed across the shifting, unstable junk piles. On the far wall, he spied the bottom of their living room couch, the solid oak and red velvet one his mother had been so proud of. Henry grabbed one end in his soot-covered hands and used all his strength to flip the heavy couch right side up. To his surprise, it flipped right over, and he nearly tumbled backward onto the twisted shards of blackened wood and pipes. Half of the couch had been burned away, leaving only the charred frame—and that broke neatly in half when Henry turned it.

Henry ran his fingers along the single remaining red velvet cushion and remembered his mother's voice all those years ago, warning him to stay off that couch, that it was for guests, that it was hard enough having nice things without a boy getting his dirty hands all over everything. Exhaustion swept over him, and he laid down, his head on the cushioned red velvet arm of the half-burned couch, his legs on the rubble. He slept all day, and no one knew he was even there.

St. Mary's Cemetery in Appleton a week later, a gloriously warm late April afternoon. Father Michael put his hand on Henry's shoulder and told him his parents were in heaven, smiling down on him, and even though he missed the funeral, they knew he would have been there if he could. Henry thanked him for this second, private memorial service and for the church putting up the money for the small headstone.

And then Father Michael left Henry standing there alone.

The setting sun reflected off the gravestones that were scattered along the hill above the Fox River. The first dusty blooms of cherry and daffodil had broken out, and the cemetery was dotted with color. Henry found himself walking among the dead-on gravel lanes and along the cart paths. Then he made his way west and south until he was out of the cemetery and walking down Prospect Avenue. At the railroad crossing, he left the road and hiked south down the tracks on his way back to Menasha, although he didn't really know why he should go back there at all. The room he was renting was tiny and faced the paper mill in Racine. The pulp stench and constant noise made it a terrible place to find some peace. And besides, with his Army discharge pay, he could afford much better.

He walked along the tracks thinking of the places he could go, but nothing at all appealed to him. He even considered reenlisting with the Army, but then visions of dead and dying soldiers and civilians flashed into his mind and almost knocked him over.

He hiked south for an hour, a slow amble into the gathering darkness, and reached the point just west of the trestle that crossed the lake from the west side over to Menasha, the place where that branch line joined the main north-south track. A nearly full moon rose above the mills on the Menasha side and sparkled the lake with silver pearls of light.

In the distance from the north, he heard the high-pitched whistle of a steam engine crossing at Prospect a few miles back. He stepped off the tracks and looked north. Around a bend in the distance, a white headlight came into view. Three locomotives belched black smoke into the sky and pulled dozens of tankers filled with limestone slurry followed by flat cars piled high with timber from the north woods. He let his eyes go out of focus as the cars flashed rhythmically in front of him.

Then he saw something strange. At first, he thought it was an illusion, a trick of the dusk, sparks off the tracks somehow.

Then he was sure of it.

As each car passed, he caught a glimpse of the dark forest on the other side of the train. Standing at the edge of the woods was a woman. Henry was sure of it. He looked north, but the end of the train was nowhere in sight. He dropped to his hands and knees and peered under the cars to get a longer look at what might be there.

Against the darkness of the woods, he saw the lower half of a woman's body, her legs wrapped in a long, brown skirt, standing with her hands folded at her waist. The train rolled on, but the woman did not move. Henry stood again and watched her in the narrow gap that flashed past between cars. She seemed to stare at him intently. Her long brown hair fell in a thick braid across her brown shirt that was studded with colorful beads.

He looked north. Twenty cars to go.

He closed his eyes and remembered the woman he met on patrol in the hills near the North Korean border. An American air raid had softened up the area, and Henry's platoon was moving in to clean it up. Routine all the way. She had hair just like that, long and brown, and her eyes sparkled. She held a ball out in front of her as if she wanted to play. She was calling out to someone, but Henry saw nobody nearby. She was so out of place, smiling at him, happy to see him in this terrible place, that Henry thought he was dreaming her. As he walked toward her that hot morning, the dust from the air raid settling on the forest like dew, he thought she was laughing, holding her arms out to him, offering that child's toy to him, like she had stepped right out of this lonely young soldier's dreams. Then, as he reached out for her, smiling himself, as if he had found a kindred spirit so far from home, she fell to her knees, then face first onto the ground. Her back was stained red where shrapnel had cut through her clothes. Blood soaked through her pants along the backs of her legs and into Henry's uniform when he scooped her up and ran to find help.

The medic in Henry's unit said she was dead before she hit the ground.

Visible through the windows of the caboose, the train crew played cards by lamplight. Their bored faces, eyes half closed, flashed past Henry and down the tracks.

Henry's mind adjusted to the return of darkness and to the silence. Behind him in the swamp between the tracks and Little Lake *Butte des Morts*, spring peepers croaked and whistled at the return of warmer weather.

There, across the tracks, stood the woman, her arms still folded at her waist. Henry didn't move. She was beautiful, this woman. Dark skin, dark eyes, dark hair.

Then, silently, she started toward him.

She stepped over the tracks and walked to his side.

Henry couldn't breathe.

When she touched his cheek, it was as if all the heat went out of his body. He pulled away sharply, and the woman pulled her hand back, covering her mouth. He saw in her eyes that she was sorry.

They stood together, face to face, for what seemed like hours. Henry was not afraid, although he knew very well that this was no ordinary woman. But something told him that she meant him no harm. For some strange reason, he felt safe with her. Finally, he thought of the reason why: this woman, impossible as it seemed, reminded him of his mother. It wasn't anything physical, even though this woman and his mother were about the same age. More than that, she looked like a soldier's mother whose son had gone off to fight in a faraway place.

Compassion welled up in Henry's breast. He would stay out there in the woods for as long as she needed him. After all, he had nowhere to go.

Finally, the woman spoke. Her voice was soft and distant, and her strange-sounding words tumbled out across the silent night. Her voice was filled with love but barbed along the edges with what sounded to Henry like desperation. Henry understood none of it, but he nodded with compassion. He wanted to understand. She gestured down the branch line toward the trestle across the lake. She motioned for Henry to follow her. He did.

No more than fifty feet down the tracks, she stopped. Henry reached her side. Wordlessly, she crouched to the ground. She pointed emphatically at a small white stone. Puzzled, Henry reached for it.

He touched the stone.

Sudden, powerful visions tore through his mind—pain, suffering, gunshots in the night, a surprise attack, blood everywhere, bodies along the riverbank, in the trees, screams of agony.

Abandoned.

Lost.

Years.

Henry dropped the stone and fell to his knees. The visions vanished. He rubbed his eyes and looked up at the woman. She knelt next to him, careful not to touch him. She pointed at that stone and then another just like it. This time, Henry didn't touch anything. He just looked. In the moonlight, he saw that it was flat and pocked with holes.

That was no stone, Henry realized.

It was a bone. Animal? Maybe a deer?

By the shape of it, part of a skull.

But those visions, the agony he felt when he touched the bone. What was that?

He looked up at the woman. Tears streamed down her cheeks in the moonlight as she pressed her hands against her breast. She raised her eyes to the sky and made the saddest sound Henry had ever heard, a wail that carried out across the lake to the Menasha mills beyond.

Are they human bones?

Henry put his hand down on the ground to lever himself up, but when his hand touched the ground, a new vision tore through his mind—sickness, fever, a small child in his mother's arms, long dead, buried, but now... what? Painfully awoken out here in the night, the child, confused, looking again for his mother, the fever turning branches of the trees into ferocious monsters looming overhead. The child crying out a name again and again, a name Henry knew must mean, "Mother!"

The woman gestured all around them. Then Henry saw them—shards of white bone littered along the railroad tracks on the raised grade that met the trestle fifty yards to the east. Shards of bone mixed with the gravel of the rail bed. The bodies of centuries of the dead and buried churned up to the surface when the railroad went through.

Bodies everywhere, their spirits in agony, screaming out for peace and for rest.

Henry reached out to the woman. Ghosts, these were, here among their unburied bones, here, a hill of the dead. When Henry touched her, she opened her eyes and looked at him hopefully.

She reminded him of his mother whom he could not save.

In this woman's eyes was a plea for help. Maybe he could do something for her.

Late sunny May, and a bent, thin young man walked along the railroad tracks slowly, his eyes intently scanning the ground between the ties and along the embankment. Every few feet he stopped and picked up something small and dropped it into a leather bag slung from his shoulder.

Henry's face was well sunburned, and he had lost a lot of weight from his already skinny physique. He moved slowly and deliberately, stopping every few feet to pick something up. Sometimes, he would stiffen, as if he were being jolted by electricity, but he dutifully dropped another white stone into his bag before moving on.

The sun dipped low in the western sky and Henry left the train tracks and walked down a thin path through the underbrush. Twisting through the brambles and thorns, he made his way to a pile of freshly turned dirt. He took the bag from his shoulder and loosened the tie. He dumped the white pebbles onto the dirt pile reverently.

Then he picked up a shovel and cut into the ground nearby. He brought a blade full of wet loam and clay and let it fall onto the bones. He piled up more and more dirt until the mound had grown by another few inches.

Day after day it had been like this. The woman had not returned, but why would she? Henry knew what needed to be done.

He reached down and touched the newly piled dirt. As if from a great distance, he heard exhaling, sighs of relaxation. He imagined the spirits of the restless dead finding peace in this mound, buried again finally after so long.

Once a week, Henry walked south into Neenah to buy bread and sausage to keep him going. The June day was unseasonably cool, and a misty rain fell from low clouds. Henry crossed the street to the market. Before he reached the door, someone called out, "Henry!" A man gestured to him to follow him behind the store. In a daze, Henry obliged. It had been weeks since he had heard his own name.

When he rounded the corner, he saw the market manager, old Mr. Hesser. Henry's mother used to shop at this market, and Mr. Hesser used to tousle Henry's hair, calling him Sport. Now he had a smile on his face, but Henry could tell it was not a happy one. "Look here, Henry. I've got a box all packed for you. Your usual stuff, plus a few treats."

Henry looked at him and frowned. "You packed this for me?"

"Sure thing, son. And put your money away. It's on me. You've had a rough time of it, we all know. It's the least I can do for you and your dear departed parents. And I'll leave your box of supplies out here for you every Tuesday just like this. Save you time."

"No need, sir. I kind of like shopping, picking out what I want. It's the only—"

"See here, Henry. That won't do. It just won't do," he rubbed his hands nervously against his apron. "Look, son, I have to be honest with you. You're bothering the customers. You haven't had a bath since when? Your clothes—they're all, well, you look like you need a good hosing down, that's all. And talking to yourself... You're scaring people. Aw, shucks, son, see it from my side. I've got a business to run," he said and reached out to touch Henry's shoulder. "It's nothing personal—agh!" He pulled his hand away from where he had lightly brushed Henry's shoulder. He stumbled back against the building with his hand against his chest. "You stay right there. Don't come any closer. What the hell was that?"

Henry felt his skin tighten under the touch, felt the familiar restless spirits coursing through his veins like fire. But how could he explain it to Mr. Hesser? How could he explain it to anyone?

The world of the living, right here in front of him, called out. But the hill of the dead called to him strongly, too. What did he owe to those restless spirits out there along the tracks?

What did he owe to nice old Mr. Hesser?

He looked over the old man's shoulder into the parking lot of the shop where several customers had stopped to see what was happening. Mr. Hesser himself cleared his throat uncomfortably.

Henry turned to look out across the water to where the trestle crossed the lake, where the building of the rail line had exhumed the countless dead. One world or the other, and Mr. Hesser wanted him to decide at that moment.

What was it going to be?

Henry closed his eyes and saw his mother, her face lined and careworn, the very last time he had ever seen her. He could not save her. The young mother in Korea, too. Too late to save her, he was indirectly responsible for her death. But now maybe, just maybe, he could help somebody else's mother.

He thanked Mr. Hesser, lifted the box filled with food, and trudged down Main toward Lake Street. He walked north to the crossing of the main north and south train line. He left the road and entered the woods between the rails, skipping from tie to tie, the voices of the restless dead becoming stronger within him as he got closer and closer to the trestle and the edge of Little Lake *Butte des Morts*.

The late August sun beat down upon Henry's back. His tattered shirt hung limply across his shoulders. He clambered along the embankment only a few feet from the lakeshore. He carefully extracted tiny bone fragments that were lodged among the gravel. The worn leather bag bounced lively at his side. He finished combing the embankment by late morning and began a second sweep while working his way west toward his ever-growing mound.

Beneath his feet, the earth was silent, at rest. No more sharp, painful memories. No more screams of terror in his mind. Just stones and dirt.

After noon, he found nothing more: no more shards of white bone bleached by the sun, snow, and rain, no more pieces of the long-dead exhumed by the railroad's steam shovels as they broke into the graves of those killed in the massacre on the Fox River so long ago.

One last time, he buried the bones in the woods. He buried the tattered leather bag, too, making sure to smooth out the dirt on top of the hill of bones.

The afternoon sun, brilliant in the western sky, the day still hot but his work complete, Henry walked out to the middle of the trestle, far out above the lake, removed his tattered, muddy clothes, and leaped out into the air, his arms outstretched, eyes closed. He felt the blistering heat of the sun on his fragile body. He shouted as he fell, tried to match the sad wail of the woman, and as he entered Little Lake Butte des Mortes, he let go of the grief for his parents, the soothing, cold water washing it all away, the dirt, the blood, the years, even his grief. He let go of the sadness of the woman, too, and knew that in his life at least he had helped one person to set things right.

HAUNTING THE DOCTOR'S WIFE

Sometime around 1899, a young Chicago doctor and his wife moved into an old stone lakefront house in Neenah. A few months after the couple arrived, the wife—a beautiful, young, stylish woman who had trouble making friends in the lonely northeast Wisconsin manufacturing outpost—began to tell of strange doings in that old stone house while her husband worked. The frightened young wife told of pots and pans flying through the air for no good reason, food being dumped all over the kitchen by a phantom, clothes being torn to shreds by unseen hands.

Finally, after a harrowing winter spent watching their possessions slowly destroyed by the poltergeist on the lake shore, the doctor and his wife packed what remained of their belongings and booked train passage back to Chicago. At the Neenah train station, those seeing them off reported that the doctor had a serious look on his face, that he apologized to his patients for having to leave them so soon. Those same witnesses reported that the wife, on the other hand, flashed an inscrutable smile as she stood alone on the platform, her luggage stacked neatly at her side. Most agreed that they were happy to see her on the road to recovery so quickly after such an awful, terrifying year in the old, haunted stone house on Lake Winnebago's shore.

A MILLION YEARS TILL MORNING

Den washed his hands; the cold water cascaded onto the dull white porcelain of the dairy farmer's battered kitchen sink.

He scrubbed the dirt from under his fingernails and rinsed them clean.

He shut off the water and looked through the dirty window westward where the August sky had almost completely darkened.

Night.

A million years till morning.

Time enough to sleep before the next milking at four.

If he could sleep.

He needed to find a way to make it stop.

Three months now since the funeral, and he hadn't slept, not really.

His mind spun.

Every muscle quivered with exhaustion.

He moved automatically, shutting off the light in the dark, cold kitchen. He wiped his hands while he walked to the hallway.

Three months.

He had settled into a routine of desperate silence and grave action, plodding ahead with a solitary farmer's life, something he thought he had wanted all along.

With Louise alive and sick as she had been for years, their lives had an unpredictability Den just couldn't abide.

And he told her often, chastised her for moaning aloud in pain and for complaining about the suffering she said she was feeling.

Truth was, she had been ill for so long, Den never knew what was real and what was imagined.

Sometimes, he believed that it was all a hysterical illness, that she was just tired of the work on a farm and looked for an easy way out.

At times during the past few years, he regretted their marriage.

She was the prettiest girl in Little Chute and all the boys wanted to date her, but she chose Den above all the others.

And when the prettiest girl in town chooses you, well, there is not much to say other than yes, is there?

But she wasn't much of a farmer's wife.

She never took to the routine, the long days, the demanding physical labor.

She read her books and magazines and asked Den if they'd ever travel to places like Paris or Rome or New York.

Why would an udder jockey from Wisconsin want to spend days on a crowded train just to go to some overcrowded, crime-filled city?

What did they have that Little Chute didn't?

They could go to shows in Appleton or Oshkosh, stay at fine hotels, eat thick steaks—why did they need to travel halfway around the world to do the same thing at ten times the price?

And besides, who'd take care of the stock even for a day?

No, Louise was a dreamer—and he told her so.

Told her to get her mind back to farm life and put away those magazines, his index finger pounding out every other syllable.

They were just putting grand ideas into her head, and he'd have none of it.

Never do her any good, anyway. Just made her dreamy and soft.

Den stood at the foot of the stairs in the failing daylight and wiped his damp hands across his pants.

He closed his eyes.

A strange quiet out here in a big, empty house.

He waited.

Then he heard it.

Not again, he whispered. Please. Have mercy.

Coming from upstairs, the sound of footsteps.

Unmistakable.

There's a person up there, Den knew.

And no one was within a mile of the house, not this late in the day.

The sound came from up the stairs toward the back bedroom.

If only it were a thief.

Den's bird gun could solve that problem.

If only.

Den climbed the stairs and walked purposefully to the back bedroom, the one he used to share with Louise.

He stood outside the bedroom door, which was slightly ajar.

From inside, he heard someone humming a sweet melody.

A woman's voice.

He nudged open the door with his toe.

She stood with her back to him at her dresser.

She leaned down and placed something Den couldn't see into the bottom drawer.

That dress.

The dark hair flowing like ivy down her back.

Then she turned.

Den leaped back at the sight of her.

"Not again," he hissed desperately.

He held his head in his hands.

Dead and buried, she was.

Dead and buried.

"Stay away!" he whispered hoarsely. "Leave me be."

But what could he do?

He needed sleep.

He peeked back into the room; she was gone.

The thing that looked like her was gone.

"A devil it was, sent here to drive me insane. I'll have none of it."

Den was a good Lutheran and knew the sight of the devil when he came around.

Came in the guise of a loved one to lead him astray.

He searched the room, opened the closet door; the light in the bedroom lit the small space dimly, his few forlorn shirts limp and gray.

Gone.

He placed the lamp on the bedstand and undressed.

No time for seeing things.

Time for sleep.

He felt the first stirrings of autumn through his bare feet as he climbed into the cold bed.

He blew out the lamp.

He rested his head and thought about Louise, her gentle touch, her cold feet, her body pressed against his.

Dreamy and soft—he spat those words at her like a curse.

He had been mistaken about those words, he knew now.

But far, far too late.

He drifted off to sleep.

Soon, however, he emerged from a dream and lay still, hardly breathing.

There, on the edge of the bed, silhouetted by moonlight, sat Louise.

Her skin shimmered, alive, glistening, as if she had absorbed all the moonlight in the world until she overflowed with it.

She turned to him, her eyes searching, hopeful.

Her lips moved silently, mouthing happy words, enthusiastic.

So young, she looked, Den thought.

Lovely.

Den had forgotten how radiant she once was, her old self, before the cancer, how when he looked at her, he felt as if she were falling face first through warm air onto something softer than rain.

She held up her hand as if to show him something.

Nothing.

Den saw nothing.

That was the story of their lives together.

They saw different wonders.

Ignoring him, she laughed and pressed her hands to her breast, turned to him and smiled sweetly.

Den whispered, "Louise!" reached out for her, but in an instant, she was gone, faded into the moonlight that angled through the dusty windowpane.

Den rubbed his eyes.

Maybe it's over for tonight, he thought. Maybe tonight I'll get some sleep.

He felt like he had a cannonball in his throat.

The full moon overhead streamed white light onto the sill when Den next stirred.

He opened his eyes warily, unsure whether he was sleeping or dreaming.

There at her dresser, her back to him, stood Louise, or, rather, the devil that looked like her.

Have mercy on me, Den prayed quietly.

Have mercy.

She peered closely at her face in the mirror, pulling and poking at the skin around her eyes.

Den used to chide her as he lay down to sleep, called her vain, quoted Bible verses about pride and hellfire, told her to turn off the light so he could sleep.

But now, now, for three months now, he simply watched her.

The curves of her hips and long legs under the nightgown he had given her last Christmas.

A hairbrush, a hand mirror, a small jewelry box that she used less and less as the years passed.

Her thin arms, the graceful line of her neck.

Lines of worry that creased her forehead, cheeks, and chin.

She aged years in the minute he watched.

She became fragile, her eyes distant and dim.

She pressed her hands to her ears in pain, her mouth screaming silently at the nothingness in the mirror.

Den put his hands over his ears.

She swept her arm across the top of the dresser, but nothing moved.

Nothing moved.

The same thing every night, this dream, this hallucination, this visitation.

The same thing every night.

Den's mind felt as if it would shatter.

He tried to breathe.

He tried to stop breathing.

He pressed the sheet to his face and said, stop, stop, stop, stop, stop...

Tap.

He must have slept for a while.

Tap.

He had the sense that the sound had started long before he was fully aware of it.

Tap.

He lay still in bed and listened.

Someone was tapping on the door, on the floor, on the walls, all around him, it seemed.

Bang.

It grew louder.

The bathroom—that's where it came from.

Inside the bathroom.

Bang!

This has happened before, he thought, untangling the sheets and stumbling across the cold floor.

He reached for the door handle.

Boom!

The thunder, up close, shook the door frame.

He turned the knob.

Inside, he saw Louise—the ghost of Louise, a demon, whatever—leaning hard against the sink, two hands, elbows bent, her back arched, contractions rippling through her small body.

Her mouth opened, as if to vomit, but nothing came out.

Dry heaves, the last month of her illness.

More than once, he had accused her of making herself sick.

Accused her in anger that his sleep had been disturbed.

Angry that she again would not help him with chores.

Instead, she asked for his help.

For weeks and weeks, she asked for his help.

He responded with ridicule and derision.

And tonight, the ghost of her turned to him again.

He felt like his body would break, that his mind would crack like ice on a deep-frozen lake.

The ghost of her turned to him and pleaded wordlessly for help. Her mouth twisted in anguish, a smear of blood on her upper lip, her eyes desperate with pain and fear.

She screamed at him, lunged at him to push him out of the bathroom.

He opened his arms to embrace her, to hold her up, to support her.

Den felt nothing at all when her arms passed through him.

She wiped her mouth, ran fingers through her ragged hair, and hunched over the sink.

Den remembered the night.

She had pushed him out of the bathroom, told him she hated him, told him she was dying, and he didn't care, was likely glad of it.

He clenched his eyes tight.

She had pushed him out of the bathroom.

Had locked the door against him.

In his own house.

And she was so sick.

He followed her image into the bedroom.

He knew where she was going, where she would sit, remembered it all, her eyes vacant, empty, at the edge of the bed.

Her body shook with fever.

Den shouted, "Please!"

He held his hands to his ears remembering that night.

It was all too much.

But for three months the night played out like a stuck machine, a photo, a still life.

That night, when he shattered the door frame with his shoulder, sent shards of wood flying through the air.

His Louise—she chose him above all the other men in Little Chute—he grabbed her by the arm—that frail, weak twig—and tossed her out of the bathroom, said he had to go, and he'd be damned if he'd go outside into the cold.

He used the toilet and went back to bed.

Ignored her, even as she stayed in that bathroom the rest of the night vomiting.

Ignored her.

His Louise.

Tonight, the image of her stood by the bed, used the post to steady herself, waited for him to be finished, lifted her eyes to look confidently, defiantly, at the bathroom door where he remembered walking out that night, bustling past her, and getting under the covers with a pillow over his head.

He didn't know that for a long time she had stood next to the bed, right above him, as he fell asleep.

Den's chest heaved watching it all again.

How could he have fallen asleep?

How could he have been so weak?

The farmer's life, was that it?

She reached out for him, her thin fingers stroking air above the mounded blankets.

"Wake me!" Den shouted, his mind spinning in anguish.

She stood above him, her body nearly broken by pain and illness and worse.

"Wake me!" he hissed.

He staggered to her side, put his face close to hers.

"Wake me!" he screamed. "Please!"

It was as if he were the ghost.

She pulled her hand back and turned toward the bathroom, resigned, defeated.

"Wake me!" Den cried. "Louise!"

For a moment, she hesitated. Turned toward him, and with a queer look in her eyes, reached out.

"I'm here," Den whispered, groping toward her in the moonlight.

"I'm still here!"

She turned from the bed and faced Den, the real, living Den, and stared at him, through him. With a curious, confused look on her face, she reached out a hand toward him.

Her hand, immaterial, passed through Den, left no impression.

She closed her eyes, breathed deeply, and walked past him, into the bathroom.

She closed the broken door as best she could.

Den slumped to the floor against the bed frame.

For three months now, he couldn't find the strength to go in there with her.

He knew what waited for him, what she did that night because he knew what he had found the next morning.

Every night for three months, the same.

Every night.

And still, he could not face what waited for him in there.

It might take a million years of nights like this.

A million years till morning.

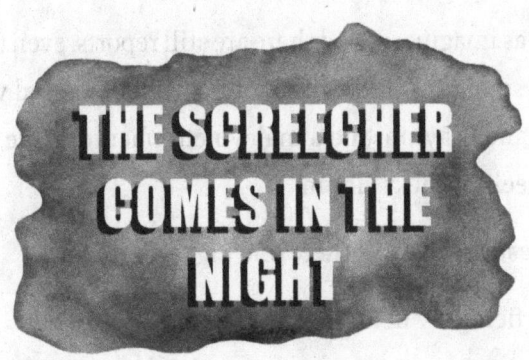

THE SCREECHER COMES IN THE NIGHT

You overhear hushed talk on the playground, under the slide, and, later, by the great pipe that dumps rainwater into the lake. A whisper: "Did you hear it last night?" You nod, solemn, quick, turn your eyes away. Some kids say it's a ghost. Others say it's a lost cousin of humans, a giant ape-like ancestor, something like Bigfoot: carnivorous, merciless, immortal. Parents don't hear the unholy screech the thing makes—they never know about real things—and when you try to tell them, they say, "Go back to sleep!" or "It was just a dream." You find a book in the library that tells you that the early white settlers just west of what is now called Neenah knew exactly what the creature sounds like: in the deep heart of the night, a high-pitched moan, a scream, not human, followed by a terrifying grunt as heavy footfalls like distant thunder crash through the brush. The book says that on some mornings farmers find huge animal prints in the mud near their lonely house. They kick dirt and snow over them so the wife and kids won't start talking about moving south to a place where the Screecher couldn't track them by their human scent. That's what those early white settlers called the beast, the Screecher. Check the papers from that time—kids went missing, dogs and livestock, too. No explanation but for the strange noises reported, dismissed as imaginary. And there are still reports, even to this day, of strange sounds in the night coming from fields and woods out by Larsen and Clayton, and a malevolent phantom, the specter of fear, as it seeks its next victim.

Go ahead—drive out there one night.

Find a field, any field, shrouded in mist.

Shut down the headlights and the engine, if you dare.

Then wait.

If you see a strange glow in the distance that seems to be coming closer, if the night itself takes on an eerie cast, greenish, menacing, if you hear something unearthly out at that field, a high-pitched moan you just can't place, something terrifying, and if it is coming closer and closer in the night, drawn by the heat of your body, the smell of the blood coursing through your veins, I have one piece of advice for you:

Run!

Get away from there as fast as you possibly can.

And don't look back.

The Screecher comes in the night!

INCIDENT AT THE VULCAN MILL

Jack locked the office door and crept across the darkened mill floor. His job as foreman was to make sure everyone was out, and the machines were safely shut off before locking up the building for the weekend. He'd been working at the mill longer than any of the other men, even the bosses. On Saturday nights, Jack walked with pride among the huge pulpers and massive rollers, felt the heat of the week radiating off into the silent night air as if the mill itself died every weekend, gave up its ghost into the early Sunday morning darkness.

Jack rested his hand against a huge roll of paper. This is my mill, he thought. Every machine, as if I designed them myself. He looked around. Such a noisy place during the day gave him shivers at night by being so deathly quiet. A good place for the devil to play with a man's mind. But he'd be busy elsewhere, Jack grunted. These young men who think they know it all: what do they know? Sinners, every one of them. Let them have their fun, Jack thought. I'll crush them on Monday morning, me, an old man, teaching them what hard work really means.

His check complete, he stepped out into the moonless, cold night. He gave the door handle one last tug to make sure it had locked right and gingerly made his way down the stairs. All it would take is one patch of black ice, and Jack's night would end with broken bones. He pulled his hat down to cover his ears and turned up his collar as he walked carefully down the path along the Fox River. The last streetcar of the night had departed long ago, so he had to walk home. It wasn't far—he didn't mind. In fact, he preferred it. Most men went out to the saloons after work, especially on Saturday. They'd be drinking and dancing, with painted ladies all over them, until dawn. Then they'd slink stinking drunk back to their dingy homes, their week's pay gone, their minds blasted to bits. Not Jack. He was better than that, better than those men. He saved his money, kept his body clean. He went home to his big, empty house, the same one he grew up in. Let those stupid, young men debauch themselves, ruin their lives. Jack was a good Christian man. He'd stay at home and out of trouble.

In the distance, he heard the lonely howl of a steam train, then the backfire of a Model T. Jack shook his head. Streetcars take you anywhere you want to go. Why anyone would waste their money on a car was beyond him.

But then he stopped. That train whistle. Strange. No mills were up and running at this time of Saturday night. No trains, either, would be rolling. Who'd be there to accept a delivery?

He listened in the still night air. Another blast of the whistle. It was definitely running south down the Wisconsin Central line, and it was getting closer. And unless he was mistaken, it was rolling down the Fox River trunk, rolling from the west down the line to the Vulcan Mill.

He looked up the hill toward his house and thought about the warm bed that waited for him. But if there was a delivery coming to the mill, he'd best be there to receive it, even at this late hour. He pulled his hat lower onto his head and walked back down the hill toward the river.

The Vulcan Mill brooded above the riverbank, its three-story brick facade nearly black against the black sky. But as he entered the gate, Jack saw something unexpected—there it was! In a window on the top floor, a faint yellow light flickered.

"That can't be!" Jack whispered to himself.

He walked to the door, his keys jingling in his hand. His numb fingers couldn't grasp the keys right. A cold wind cut through the night, shivered through his clothing.

The train whistled again—this time, much closer. The key finally slipped into the lock.

Jack found the lamp he had extinguished only a few minutes before. It was cold to the touch. He lit the wick and opened the hood up to full flame.

He hurried down the hallway past the offices of the managers. There, at the end of the hall, light filled a glazed glass door pane. The train whistle blew again, closer still, the low rumble of steel wheels on rails, common enough during the day so that no one noticed it, obtrusive and loud only when everything else stopped for Sunday.

Jack knocked at the door meekly. Silly. There'd be no one up here in the bookkeeping office at this time of night. He tried the lock. It opened in his hand. That's not good, he thought. These were supposed to be locked up tight. How had he missed it? Maybe he was slipping, losing his mind. Maybe that was it.

Jack pushed open the door, disoriented. Nothing was as it should be. It certainly was warm in this office, for one thing. He walked over to the desk where the lamp still blazed bright. Good thing he found it, Jack thought. This kind of carelessness could get the whole mill burned down.

On the desk, he couldn't help but see the headline: "Hundreds Burned in Fire at Peshtigo." Jack wasn't much of a reader, but he made his way through the first paragraph. The whole town burned, it said. Most everyone died. He leaned closer and started the second paragraph. The flames had moved so quickly that no one could even outrun the inferno.

The train's whistle blasted so shrilly that Jack almost leaped onto the desk in fright. When he could breathe again, he turned to the window that looked out over the stockyard and the Fox River, an inky void, beyond.

There, in the stockyard, as if by some kind of magic, a locomotive hissed and rolled slowly to a halt. It was a giant, black locomotive, its coal tender black and scaly like a dragon's tail. It had pulled one bulkhead flatcar of timber into the stockyard.

That'd be a delivery, Jack thought. But only a single load of timber? Hardly worth a trip to a mill that processes a dozen loads like that every day.

A shadowy figure hopped down off the locomotive, fell to the dirt, struggled to his feet, and vanished behind the train. Jack tried to call out, but the words caught in his throat. He wicked off the bookkeeper's lamp and walked down the hall holding his own lantern in front of him to guide him through the darkness.

He wanted to be angry, to be tough and strong, but late at night when his legs stiffened painfully and his memory wandered, Jack really felt his age. He wished the delivery had not come. He wished he was already home, a ready-made excuse. He thought for a moment about running but then grunted. Run? From what? This is my mill. And no one can just drop off a load like that whenever they want to. There's paperwork to be done.

Outside again, through the mill yard gate, he poked his head around the front of the locomotive and spotted a man standing at the back of the timber flatcar. Jack called out, "Hey! What the hell is going on here?"

The man emerged slowly from between the cars and regarded Jack warily.

Jack stopped where he was. There was something disturbing about the man. A long black coat covered him from head to toe, but his face, even in the lantern light, had a deathly pallor to it, as if all the blood had been drained out of him.

Jack shouted, "What do you mean by coming here after midnight?"

The man in black took a step toward Jack and held up both hands toward him. His palms were as black as the night sky.

That stopped Jack. "What is this, anyway?" Jack asked, trying to sound confident.

"I have to—" the man in black stammered. "I can't go on..." his voice trailed off into the night.

The river in mid-autumn runs high and rolls over the little mill dams loudly, but that's not the sound Jack studied at that moment. He walked warily to the flatcar of new timber. Could it be that they hissed softly, as if wind was blowing through the branches of the trees they used to be? But that couldn't be. They had no branches, and the night air was still.

Something made him want to touch the piled wood, but he snatched his hand away quickly. These logs were red hot, as if they were on fire.

But they weren't on fire. They showed no signs of combustion. Jack could smell only the heat. A pile of dark, scorchingly hot logs hissed into the night air.

"You going to explain this?" he said in wonder to the man in black. But when Jack looked up, the man had vanished. Jack shook his head. Too often lately he saw things or heard things that were not there. This was like a dream somehow.

The sound of the brake being released on the locomotive snapped him back to reality. He swung onto the lowest step of the ladder and hoisted himself up into the locomotive, where the man in black was stoking the coal fire.

"What are you doing?" Jack demanded with a voice more confident than he felt.

The man turned to him and sighed. "It's yours now. I have done all I can." He went back to stoking the fire and building pressure on the boiler.

But Jack knew how to stop him, and from the look of the man in black, he couldn't overpower even an old man. Jack lunged forward, grasped the brake, and pulled it hard. "You're not going anywhere until I get some answers. Tell me what the hell is going on."

The man shut the coal door and let his head sag, exhausted. "You can't keep me here."

Jack gestured toward the brake handle, "Yes, I can."

The man in black swallowed hard. "If I tell you, will you take them in?"

"Who?" Jack whispered.

"The survivors," the man in black replied.

Jack shook his head. "I don't understand."

The man in black looked outside into the darkness and spoke softly: "Six days ago, I was working the Peshtigo line, hauling timber cars from the north woods to main line depots. Then the devil himself breathed across the land, and it all burned. I was there, this one single engine stoked and full steam when the fire hit. It came so fast I scarcely escaped. People along the rails I passed," the man in black rubbed his forehead as if in pain, "begged me to stop to let them get aboard. Families, children, old people. But the flames barreled down those tracks nearly as fast as I could roll. I slowed, tried to grab onto some of the stronger ones as I passed, but I couldn't hold on from up here..."

Jack steadied himself.

"I looked back to see my coal tender on fire, but what could I do? More and more people threw themselves onto the loaded bulkhead flatcar back there. I slowed again so that maybe more of them could latch on, but for every one that held somehow, four or five slipped off the back and tumbled behind me down the tracks, screaming in anguish as the fire ate them alive. I hit the hill too slow, and the fire caught me. The whole flatcar ignited and all that timber with all those people just went up all at once. I tell you, I put my head down, said the best prayer I knew, and let the engine rip. Just let me save a few of those poor people, I prayed. Just a few of them. I felt the flames at my back as we sped up that hill and down the other side. The screams—that's what sticks with me. The screams as all those people burned alive. I rolled on and on for days. And I can't go on." He looked at Jack with death in his eyes. "You must make sure—you must promise me—to safeguard this timber. Don't let anyone near it, don't let anyone touch it. I know what I'm talking about. Believe me. I know. Please promise me."

Jack fingered the brake. "What's in it for me?" he growled.

"I can't go any farther. I feel it coming for me, too. The fire!" The man in black staggered toward Jack, his gnarled arms reaching out like hooks.

Jack scampered down the ladder and fell to the ground, pushing himself backward on his feet and hands. Far above him, the man in black leaned out of the locomotive. "Promise me you will leave these souls in peace for as long as it takes."

Jack whispered, "I promise," but scarcely knew what he was saying.

Far above him, the man in black ducked back into the locomotive. Steam filled the pistons, and the train came alive again. It chugged eastward along the Fox, toward the trestle that crossed the river at the Flats.

"Wait!" Jack shouted. The locomotive whistled shrilly into the night, a long, lonely sound, and picked up speed. Jack gave chase for a few steps but gave up. The man in black was not coming back. After a while, the train's noise faded into the night. Jack shook his head in wonder. He watched the tracks long after the last sign of the old locomotive had vanished across the river and into the forest to the east.

He stood and brushed off his clothes. Too much for one night. He wanted it all to be a trick of the mind, an illusion somehow, but when he turned, there it was, the single bulkhead flatcar piled high with timber.

Jack didn't hear anything, not really, but something told him very distinctly that he should move closer. He felt the radiating heat from the timber on his face and hands. On a cold night like this, it felt good. But as he moved ever closer, the heat became more and more intense until he had to shut his eyes and turn his face away even to breathe. But still, he moved closer. Something about it drew him in, made him want to touch it, to feel what could make this wood so hot and still not burn.

He squinted and reached his hand out to the blistering wood, his arm shaking with pain.

He wanted to pull away, but at the last moment, the force that had drawn him there grabbed him and thrust him at the wood. He fell against the timber, his arms buckling under the weight of his body, and screamed out in pain. But it wasn't exactly burning he felt.

Instead, he felt the agony of others, flames all around, watching loved ones consumed by fire, and the salvation of a single train, loaded and rolling, the desperate hope of a dying man, a woman trying in vain to save her children, the terror of a child in pain she doesn't understand. The suffering and despair of all those many, many dying people coursed through Jack, bringing violent life to his withered muscles and bones. He felt his mind coming alive as it hadn't felt in years, decades, even.

Jack roared in agony as he struggled to pull himself away from the searing wood, but at the same time, the pain felt wonderful in a way—the will to survive, the faint memory of the agony of birth.

Finally, Jack lurched away from the wood pile and stumbled across the mill yard until his head cleared. Up on his toes now, knees coiled, he was alert for that force to return. He was confident he could resist this time.

Confident, yes.

Strong, even.

Very strong.

Jack looked down at his hands. His sagging, dappled flesh had tightened up as if he were a young man again. The brown liver spots were gone. He pushed up the sleeve of his coat; the wisps of gray hair along his forearm had turned brown again somehow, exactly as they had been in his youth. He bounced up and down on the balls of his feet. Strength there, too. Great strength.

He leaped into the air and threw his arms to the sky and whooped. He hadn't felt this good in years. He flexed his arms and crouched low to the ground.

He regarded the pile of timber warily. What kind of magic was in that wood that made him feel like a new man?

He reached out to touch the wood again, and as he stepped closer, waves of searing heat again repelled him. This time, however, he was not afraid. He touched the wood and felt sweet, agonizing life coursing through his body. With both hands, he pressed against the wood.

Suddenly, all around him, the air was filled with voices, moaning and shouting incoherently. Jack pressed his forehead against the scalding logs, and the shouts drowned out all other sounds.

The pain! The pain! the voices shouted. Finally, when he could not take it anymore, he leaped backward into the cold night air and shook the heat from his burning hands. He ran back to the stockyard gate, his pants smoking, his hands singed.

The voices pursued him, screamed terribly in his ears about flaming agony and loss. Jack didn't stop to lock the gate behind him. He felt far too good, too alive to take care of such mundane responsibilities. Let the mill burn to the ground for all he cared. He was young again! And this Saturday night was young, too.

He ran joyfully to the nearest saloon, a place he never before would have considered going to. But through those doors he strode with a brashness that had been pent up for years and years and years.

The first whisky scalded his throat as it went down. The second was easier. He saw himself in the barroom mirror. It was true. He looked as young as he felt. He marveled at his face, the tight skin along his strong cheeks and chin. The dark whiskers. He still felt the warm tingle from that haunted timber, the new life that coursed through him.

In the mirror, he saw a woman sitting alone at a table near the back. She looked at him intensely, unaware that Jack was watching her, too. He found the men's room and cleaned himself up, asked for the bottle and two glasses, and made her long and pleasurable acquaintance.

When the Monday sun rose fully, and the Vulcan whistle blared across the valley— its daily wake-up whistle—Jack staggered out of bed. His head ached. He struggled to fit into his work clothes that stretched tightly over his firm muscles. Up and down the Fox River Valley, paper mills roared back to life for another week.

Jack walked out into the sunshine and thought about how he'd handle the men who had made fun of him all these years, called him an old man, told him he'd be better off dead. He opened and closed his fists and felt the explosive strength in his arms. They'd get theirs. About that, he was sure.

A harsh jingling of bells brought him back to the world. "Hey, Mister! Get out of the road!" The streetcar's brakes squealed. Jack looked back to see the Appleton trolley bearing down on him and leaped to the side of the road. The faces of the mill workers aboard gazed out at him through soot-streaked windows as they sped past. None of them recognized Jack. Up ahead, the streetcar stopped at the mill, and a group of men unfolded themselves after a hard-living weekend and trudged through the gates. He stopped to consider. No one would recognize him like this. No one would believe his fantastic story. All this time, he was counting on coming back to his foreman job. The mill did hire regularly— there was a steady flow of men in and out of jobs like that—so he figured he had a good chance to get some kind of position. But he couldn't tip his hand too soon. He knew everything about the mill, but if he showed his cards, they'd get suspicious.

Jack followed the group through the gate, careful not to stand out. The men joked and laughed in the morning sunshine. Jack followed, a minute or two behind, right on time for the start of the midday shift by the clock in the tower. He opened the front door and went to the boss's office.

Jack talked a good game. That's what the hiring man said, a young jerk who just last week told Jack to his face that he wanted him fired. "You can start immediately," the worm said with an oily smile on his face. "We need a new assistant at roller number three."

Jack thanked him and shook his soft hand so hard that the other man winced. But the effort took a little bit out of Jack. He felt his strength ebbing, felt some of his borrowed youth drain away. If only he could touch the raw timber again, to get a new dose of life.

Jack walked down the long, dark first-floor hallway and opened the back door that led directly out into the stockyard. He would tell anyone who asked that he didn't know where he was going.

The men in the mill yard worked hoists and cranes, levered timber into position onto the huge conveyor belt and onto trucks for moving into the mill.

Good so far, Jack thought. Maybe there'd be nothing, no problems at all. Jack made his way back to the sidetrack where the bulkhead flatcar had been left by the mysterious locomotive. Emerging from between piles, he came to the spot where the cars had been.

But it was all gone!

"Hey, kid." Jack used to call everyone "kid," and this youthful stockyard worker certainly merited the nickname. For a moment, Jack forgot he wasn't a foreman, forgot he was only a little bit older than this yard hand. "You see a bulkhead flatcar 'round here anyplace?"

"Sure, we got to it first thing. Lickety-split. Who's asking?"

"The timber gone now?"

The kid regarded Jack with a puzzled look as if trying to place his face. "All on the line, inside already. Here's the first load of finished product coming through," the kid jerked his thumb behind him to where a cart loaded with cut lumber was waiting to be hitched to the two horses that a bearded man steadied at the front of the cart. Jack recognized him: a furniture maker from Appleton. The kid walked over to the man and the man signed a paper the kid held out to him.

Jack walked to the furniture man's cart and stopped a few feet from the freshly cut lumber. He cringed inwardly, but he had to find out.

He reached out to touch the wood.

Cold as the air.

Jack exhaled. Maybe it all had been a dream, an illusion. He let his hand remain on the rough pine for a moment. Nothing here but—

Then he heard it. A faint voice, single, female, muted, exhausted, terrified. Then it seemed as if she recognized Jack somehow. She screamed in agony. Jack heard her being burned alive. In his mind, he saw a forest on fire, an inferno that cooked him from the outside in. He watched loved ones consumed, gasped for a breath that wouldn't scorch his lungs. Gritted his teeth so hard he felt as if his jaw would break. Still, though, the power of life, the pure will to survive at any cost, once again coursed through him. He pulled his hand away sharply and stumbled, his shoulder thudding against the side of the furniture man's cart.

It felt wonderful. Sickening, awful, terrifying—all of that. But Jack felt tingly and alive again.

He opened his eyes. The furniture man and the kid stood before him with worried looks in their faces.

Jack looked all around. He was at the Vulcan Mill, he told himself. Same as always. He was still Jack, and he lived alone in Appleton, Wisconsin. It was late October, the year 1908. He looked at his hands. Clear skin, powerful muscles, fingers that curled and uncurled whenever he wanted them to.

"Roller number three," he laughed ruefully as his head cleared. He blew into his hands. "My first day."

The kid gave him a long, searching look and shook his head. Then he slapped the rump of the furniture man's horse. The cart lurched forward with its shifting load and then rolled down the cobbled alley and out the gate, the furniture man walking beside it.

Jack knew there were more behind that, paper, lumber of all kinds, even sawdust. He walked slowly across the yard and entered the mill.

He put his hand to his chest and felt his heart pound strong and slow. The man in black told him to keep that timber safe. Jack had promised to do so. But how could he have remembered the glorious wonder of youth when it had been so long ago? How could he make a promise he didn't understand? He splashed water on his face. No, this was a fresh start, another chance at life. It had to be a good thing. The promise he made to the man in black, the agonized screams he heard coming from the timber, all of it receded behind the simple joy of strength, the chance to live life again.

He found his way to roller number three and let the morning slip by as if it were made of paper rolling endlessly. He pushed aside any thought about the rightness or wrongness of what he had done.

For the rest of the day, he operated roller number three as if in a dream. Among the milling machines, the pulpers, dryers, and rollers, making raw wood into everything a tree could become, he became conscious of a new sound. At first, he thought it was his imagination. But late in the day, he knew he could deny it no longer.

Everywhere he looked, everywhere in the mill he went, it was those same voices. They called to him, screamed in terror for his help. It was nothing anyone else could hear above the din of the workday, unless they knew what to listen for.

But Jack knew exactly what to listen for.

The terrified screams of those burned alive, voices of the dying, just out of range, part of the hiss and thump of the machinery.

They came from the timber, the lumber, from the sawdust on the floor of the mill, the dust in the air.

The voices came from everywhere.

Jack heard it, couldn't escape it, all day, the next and the next, couldn't escape it no matter where he went, the cries of the souls, trapped and burning, spirits in fiery agony, trapped now in furniture, barstools, houses, handgun grips, locked doors—everywhere he went, the screams of the dying, the anguished burning spirits whom he promised to protect.

THE DIRE EAGLES OF THE FOX RIVER

Along the Fox River during the winter, eagles hunt in the patches of open water. It is a common sight these days to see bald eagles, sometimes a dozen at a time, perched in trees or hunting among the ice floes. But there is another bird of prey active in this region, too, an elusive, nocturnal beast, twice the size of the bald eagle, difficult to spot, impossible to catch. Many people mistake it for a ghost, the silent, gray form streaking from cloud to cloud. Have you seen something like that in the winter night sky? An ornithologist friend of mine (who refused to be named here to protect his reputation) says that once a Dire Eagle reaches full maturity, it does everything any other bird does—but all of it on the wing, sometimes miles above the ground. It mates high up in the clouds—a site witnessed only by a very few baffled hot-air balloonists. It sleeps on the wing, too, circling blindly on the updrafts of warmer air.

Where do they come from, you ask, these Dire Eagles?

On the coldest day of the year, during the most ferocious winter storm, the female Dire Eagle flies thousands of feet into blizzard clouds to lay her single egg. The egg then falls through the sky, buffeted by the hurricane gales and frigid temperatures at altitude. At some point on its descent, the thick shell begins to crack. The young Dire Eagle frantically smashes its way out, racing against gravity. The young bird hatches into a blinding storm, shucking off the shell, unfurling its wings, and taking to its lifelong flight. Pieces of the shattered shell fall like hard, white flakes of snow while the fledgling beats its huge wings and rides the tempest searching for its first meal.

Like a lightning strike on a black night, a Dire Eagle drops from the sky on unsuspecting prey—geese, dogs, cats, calves, anything as warm and as alive as a human being—its talons like huge grappling hooks, its wings beating a hurricane-force downward. It vanishes back into the clouds like a ghost leaving only an absence where once the prey stood.

Spend some time outdoors along the Fox River some night this February and study the passing clouds. See a flash of dull white against the ceiling of frigid gray?

See it?

Does it look like a ghost? It very well might be.

Could it be a spotlight? An illusion?

How long are you going to stay out there by the river, anyway?

A full-grown Dire Eagle can lift a horse skyward. Do you think it would have a problem lifting you?

Still want to stay out here by the river in the dead of winter?

DIG,
HE SAID

Alice was small, had the body of a ten-year-old, but her face looked older, as if she had seen a lot for her brief years, as if the world had pushed in on her and she had long since lost the strength to push back. She wove a pattern of starts and stops down Mason Street on her way toward the forest at the south end of the street, the collection of tall trees perched on the edge of the bluff over the Fox River. She liked to watch the flowing water and to think about the wide world out there, to imagine herself paddling downstream one day like a duck free to float wherever the current took her, down past the Vulcan Mill, the flats, down through Kimberly and Little Chute, and on to Kaukauna, the rest of the world, and all the way to Green Bay.

The early spring sunlight faded as Alice passed Jefferson School, smoothing her dingy white dress. She had to keep that dress nice. No reason to give Mother another cause to be angry. She had gotten skilled at avoiding the worst of it. Today, for instance, she knew her mother sat alone at the kitchen table in a black mood. Best just to disappear, to get out of range of those fists and sharp fingernails. No sense being around to get blamed for the divorce, for her father's absence. So, she roamed the neighborhood on days like these. She liked to pretend she was invisible, a spirit in the everyday world.

Alice knew the neighborhood better than anyone else. She knew the old man who worked on his car every night. He never noticed as she watched him from behind the tree at the end of his driveway. She knew the flower garden of the mean, old woman who hated dogs, who would scream at them to stay out of her beds. Her flowers sure smelled sweet, though.

She knew the house where every day a mother stood at the stove cooking dinner for her family as a boy practiced violin upstairs. Alice stood at the end of their driveway behind the tree in the twilight and imagined someday learning to play the violin herself. She leaned against the tree, her arms bowing a phantom instrument, her fingers dancing along the neck of the violin in her mind, as elaborate, surprising harmonies meshed with the boy's simple music and took flight like a flock of geese into the wind. They would travel the world, she decided, that boy and she, giving concerts together, her curls bouncing against her shoulders as she played sweet melodies, his eyes watching her dancing hands, the crowd in rapt attention. She spun as the music in her mind moved her, she imagined her dress, long and flowing—her dress!

The tearing sound brought her back to Appleton, back to the boy's driveway. She looked down at herself with dismay. A wide tear in the cotton fabric opened up in her hand as she pulled it from where it had caught on the bark. It didn't even rip along a seam; the fabric—worn out from months of use—just shredded in her hand. She walked nervously down the block and arranged the folds of the skirt, hoping the tear would fold itself out of sight, but there it was, front and center, impossible to miss.

Alice ran the final block down to the park, to the trees, to the solitude like the end of the world to sort things out. In a dense copse of trees on the bluff overlooking the river, into the soft leafy earth she fell to her knees as tears streamed down her cheeks. She imagined how her mother would explode in anger when she saw the skirt, how nothing she could say or do would prevent the beating. And she would deserve it, too. Alice knew that. How could her mother afford to buy her a new dress? With no man in the house, they had very little money.

Maybe what she said all along was true. Maybe Alice was just a burden.

Fading daylight rose upward into the leaves, then into the clouds, the sky, and was gone.

She sat heavily on the ground and played absent-mindedly with the leaves in the twilight.

Faint, a whisper, a sound somewhere in the trees. Alice stopped moving and lifted her head. Could it be a voice she had heard? Coming from the river? There it was again! A man's voice, shouting weakly, "Help!"

Alice ran to the edge of the bluff and looked down through the thick underbrush to the river. It remained bright at sunset, the deep blue sky reflecting off the turbid spring flow. She narrowed her eyes and listened intently. There it was again! A faint whimper, a call for help, a small voice. Definitely a man's. She looked down the bluff to the bright river below. But the voice wasn't coming from that direction at all. She turned to the copse of trees behind her. Was the sound coming from there?

She walked cautiously into the trees and entered the dark, leafy room. The branches closed her inside. As her eyes adjusted, she heard the sound again, stronger this time, a single word moaned in a high, weak voice.

The voice was familiar somehow. She stepped toward the large mound of dirt and rocks as wind stirred in the treetops. Was the sound coming from under there someplace? She dropped to her knees and pressed her palms to the ground. The mound was warm. And there it was again, that faint weak voice. It was coming from there, right there. She pressed her ear to the dirt and listened intently. There it was again. Ah, she thought. Now I understand.

The voice was saying, "Dig!"

Alice stood up, alarmed. She wanted nothing more than to run home, to escape from that voice. But she stopped as she got close to the street. Something would not let her go.

She kicked at the rotting leaves left over from last fall and looked back into the dimness. The mound at the center of the trees was made of rocks and dirt. It looked out of place, now that she thought about it, that strange little hill.

That voice again! "Dig!" it whispered urgently. But the voice sounded so fragile, so distant. It was asking for help, begging for help.

Could someone be trapped under there?

That sealed her decision.

Alice smoothed the front of her dress. The sky through the leaves above her was a deep blue, unfamiliar somehow, too intense. She closed her eyes. She had to help. She just had to.

But she needed something first. She ran furtively along Mason Street toward the open garage of the man who worked on his car every night. Luckily, he and his wife were having a late dinner. She watched them as they sat silently in their kitchen. The door to the garage stood open, the old jalopy half-disassembled. She crept up the driveway and saw the neat row of garden tools that hung just inside the door. She hesitated. Stealing is wrong, she knew. But then she remembered that fragile, familiar voice calling to her. She snatched a small hand shovel and ran down the driveway and down the block. No one came after her, but still, she ran. The woman with the flower bed heard her coming and stood up from her watering, her head popping up from behind the white picket fence. Alice gasped in alarm, tried to hide the hand shovel with her body as she passed. The woman looked like she wanted to say something, but Alice kept going.

In the park, inside the quiet darkness of the room made of trees, she fell to her knees and said, "I'm back."

The voice in the dirt moaned, "Dig!" Alice cleared away the leaves covering the dirt and scratched with the shovel against the muddy dirt. Louder and louder the voice cried out, "DIG!" until

Alice was sure her whole neighborhood could hear. But she kept going, her arms and fingers moving as if on their own.

The way was not easy. Many small rocks and bits of concrete and plaster had been buried there. She dug into the side of the mound; down and in she went, carving a hole like a small cave. She had no idea how long she worked. She just kept chipping away at the pile, following the voice inside, the voice that kept shouting hoarsely, desperately, "DIG!"

And then she recognized the voice. Impossible, she knew, but unmistakable. Sweat and dirt fell into her eyes, but still she kept her fingers moving, scratching frantically at the dirt.

She did this to him, Alice thought.

Buried him alive.

She tossed a muddy rock over her shoulder.

My father was here all this time.

And she did this to him.

My mother did this.

Alice dug frantically.

Did this to my father.

Buried him alive!

Finally, her shovel hit something hard, and she used her finger to dig around it. Smoother than the other stones—and white, too. What could it be? She closed her eyes and felt the ground itself come alive somehow. The whispered word echoed inside her mind: "Dig!"

But the voice had changed.

Now it was she, herself, who said it, gasped it, through the dirt between her teeth, as darkness pressed in around her, her body inside the little cave she had dug, the air rank and humid with the smell of sweat, decay, and death.

Her father's voice gone, replaced by her own, gasping, "DIG!"

The moon rose over the park and bathed the copse of trees in silver light. All was silent in the world.

The truth was, she didn't really remember much about the night before. She waited for Alice to come home from school, but 4:00 came, and no Alice. She looked out the front window, but Alice was nowhere to be seen. Two days later, she broke down and told her neighbor. The police came and declared Alice missing, a possible runaway. She made up some harmless details about the day, told them she made a nice dinner for Alice and had tucked her in. But none of that was true. The police left, told her they'd let her know if they found anything, and Alice's mother sat alone in the kitchen and drank straight from the bottle.

She passed the third day in a haze. No Alice. At times, she thought she heard her coming up the front steps. Two more days passed. The mother grew increasingly distraught. Her sweet, little girl, Alice. "My little girl!" she shouted in anguish. She opened the cupboard and stared at the shelves, bare but for the half-empty bottle of whiskey. She ripped the bottle off the shelf and threw it across the room. "My little girl!"

The bottle smashed into a million pieces and left a brown, heart-shaped stain on the wall. She slumped to her chair and cried as the world spun around her.

The next day, the police returned and told her that they found some suspicious items in the woods at the end of Mason, and would she please come with them to see if they looked familiar.

At the park, the detective showed her the copse of trees, led her inside to the mound that had been hollowed out. They pointed to a hand shovel that lay on the ground near the pile. The mother shook her head. That shovel did not belong to her. Then they asked her to bend low, to look at the shoe prints in the dirt, and did she recognize them at all?

The woman peered at the ground in the confusion of shoe prints left by the detectives and others. Not there, he said. Over there.

She stepped carefully, adding her own to the small footprints that were everywhere in the freshly turned dirt. She recognized the worn heels of Alice's little shoes, the crack along the sole of the right shoe where the water got in when it rained.

The mother gasped in horror and fell to her knees. "Yes!" she whispered. She peered into the darkness of the cave opening. She could easily see the whole interior, could see where it had been shaped, sculpted from inside. Her eyes adjusted to the dimness inside, and she was sure she saw something else, too. For a moment, the cave became much, much deeper. For a moment, she thought she saw a small girl, her white cotton dress flashing in the dim distance.

"Alice!" the mother shouted, throwing herself at the cave opening. The little girl turned, her face a mask of anguish and suffering. A man pulled Alice by the shoulder. Just for a moment, he turned his face upward and the mother saw him, recognized him. She cupped her hands at the sides of her mouth and shouted, "Alice! Come here!"

Alice struggled against the man's iron grip. "Mother!" she screamed. "Dig!"

Her mother flung herself into the hole and scraped madly at the rocks and mud, her hands in frenzied motion, dirt flying behind her.

The detective pulled her out by her kicking legs. He radioed for an ambulance and restrained her until it arrived. All the while, the woman thrashed on the ground, screaming, "Let me up! I have to! Alice!" she shouted.

The doctor marked her as a danger to herself and others, her mind permanently clouded by grief over the death of her only child. Of course, she could not be released. Who would care for her?

Still, to this day, there is a copse of trees in Alicia Park. Despite the best efforts of the city of Appleton to bury the narrow cave opening, someone, as if drawn by some unseen force, keeps digging.

And one more thing: someone has planted flowers in the little girl's name, Alice, maintaining them for all these years as if they were in her own garden and she had watched every day as the little neighborhood girl explored her world, planned someday to talk to her, to ask her about her life, but ran out of time.

The flowers are still there.

She makes sure of it.

FREEDOM, WISCONSIN

Peter reached above the mantle and tugged at the hatchet. It didn't budge. "Get me a chair, Gertie." He ran his finger along the wood grain. He muttered, "That boy will know better by the time I'm done with him."

Gertie carried a wooden stool from the kitchen into the living room. Her new husband clambered onto it and, using leverage, rocked the blade up and down until it came loose. When it did, he wobbled, and his hand bumped the crystal clock that caught sunlight and spread diamonds from the mantle across the walls and room. He grabbed it before it fell and held it steady.

Gertie gasped and reached for it, too, her hand covering her husband's. "I really don't think it was him, Peter," she said. "I was the only one in the house and he's just a boy."

"On his way to becoming a man, and if he didn't do it, who did?"

Gertie stepped back and wiped her hands on her apron. "All the same, at least talk to him first before you do anything angry."

He gestured at the wall behind him. "It was him who got ugly first. I mean to put a stop to the next bad thing." He placed the hatchet onto the table by the window. "I won't let that boy turn into the devil his father was. Where is he?"

Gertie rubbed her eyes and remained silent.

Peter strode past her into the kitchen and out the door into the yard. "George!" He shouted. Gertie heard only the sounds of their chickens and a far-off steam train pulling another load of lumber south toward the mills in Appleton. She thought, if that boy knows what's good for him, he'll wait a good long time to show his face here again. He had friends in the city. Maybe he'd go be with them for a while.

A few weeks.

Maybe longer.

It was now clear as day that she had made such a mistake in bringing Peter into their house. He was just not suited to be a father, and George's resemblance to his deceased father was a constant reminder that he was second in her heart, had always been second. They all knew each other growing up out here, all knew the same people at the 4-H and at church. But Gertie chose gentle Arthur over the fun-loving Peter, and Peter never got over it. He was the spoiled only child of an older couple, and now that they had passed on, Peter was alone in the world. When Arthur disappeared suddenly just after his first son was born, Peter started hanging around the house more and more. One thing led to another, and twelve years later, they married.

Gertie took her apron off and sat heavily onto the sofa. She held her head in her hands and thought. That hatchet appearing where it had this morning was not the first strange thing that had happened. Only the week before, she had gone out to the milkhouse for some flour and when she returned, her cooking pot had vanished from the stove. She searched everywhere, but it had vanished. She asked George, looked him straight in the eye, if he had taken it, had hidden it as some joke. He smiled and said, "No, Mum, why would I do that?" Such a lovely smile that little boy had, like a man she once knew... And then an hour later the pot had reappeared where it had been, and still boiling? How could anyone explain that?

And yesterday while she was mending Peter's socks, the dishes that had somehow fallen from the shelves all by themselves. That's what she told Peter. One minute they were right as rain, the next they were smashing themselves to pieces on the hard floor. She was able to save some of them and hide the rest. If Peter found out they had been broken, he would be very angry. That would not do. Not at this tender moment, Gertie thought.

Her new husband's voice shouting her son's name faded as he made his way out to the barn. George's too smart to be found that easily. If he was lucky, Peter's anger would wane as it usually did, and he'd get back to work on that balky John Deere. They needed it up and running by harvest, and he was running out of time.

Then, as she sat in the living room, the hair on her neck stood up. She spun to check the window—it was closed tight. The faint aroma of something familiar entered the room, but it was a smell she couldn't quite identify, at least not immediately. She walked to the window. Outside, the yard, the barn, everything was as it should be. She tried to lift the sash, but it wouldn't budge. Then, behind her, the kitchen door slammed shut, as did the door to the stairs. She ran across the room and tried the knob. It wouldn't turn.

"Peter? This is not funny." She waited but heard only the sound of her own breathing. "George?" she whispered. "Is that you?"

Then she saw it. By the fireplace, in front of the clock he had given to her so many years before, a shadowy figure stood. He was dressed like a gentleman in a fine linen suit, his hat in his hands. His face was gentle and sweet, exactly the way Gertie remembered.

"Arthur?" she whispered in wonder.

He nodded slowly.

"Oh, George, I am so very sorry. I was out of my mind! You have to believe—."

The ghostly figure raised its arm and pointed to the table next to the sofa. On it sat a miniature painted portrait of George. Then he pointed to the mantle. He was trying to tell her something, but what was it? She walked across the room and stared at the crystal clock while the afternoon sun splashed tiny rainbows through the room.

Gertie looked back at the vision of Arthur, and his face was changing. His jaw clenched, and he bared his teeth. He held up both hands, and then blood exploded from his forehead.

Gertie screamed and collapsed onto the couch. His gentle features—she had forgotten how they drew her to him, forgotten how much she missed him, forgotten her grief on that fateful day just weeks after the birth of their first son. She had forgotten how that moment felt. She had been full of conviction that she was doing the right thing, that Arthur was—oh, she didn't know what she was thinking. Years of rationalizing had brought her no closer. If only she had hit the mantle instead.

Where that old clock sat.

It was his hobby piece. He had the tools and bought a book on clock repair. He used to spend time with it just humming softly in quiet study most nights after dinner.

Today, that clock seemed to shimmer for a moment, as if lit from inside. Gertie knew that it hadn't worked in years.

Suddenly there was a clamor outside and a door crashing open. "Get in there, you little devil!" Peter shouted. The back door crashed open, and a boy screamed. A pan crashed to the floor in the kitchen. "I mean to teach you to respect fine things. Get in there!"

George shouted, "Ma!" and tried to enter the living room, trying to escape the wrath of the man he was supposed to call father. The door was jammed shut.

Gertie ran in a panic to the door and turned the knob. The door opened smoothly. George leaped into his mother's arms. "I didn't do anything!"

Peter followed him into the living room, a crazed look in his eyes. He grabbed the boy's hair and pulled him to the floor. He pressed the heel of his boot into the boy's back and raised a thin wooden cane.

Gertie screamed, "No, Peter!" but her new husband threw her to the floor.

"You have been living off my goodness for long enough, boy. You have your father's devil inside of you!" He hit George again and again until the boy collapsed to the floor, his arms shielding the blows.

George turned upward, a crazed look in his eyes. "You'll never be my father!"

Peter grunted and kicked the boy in the side. George cried out in pain.

Gertie searched desperately around the room for something, anything. Then she saw it, exactly where Peter had dropped it earlier.

"No boy of mine would do what you do. You're the devil himself." Peter pulled George up by the hair and shoved him toward the fireplace. George crashed into the stone hearth and let out a groan. He reached up to try to stand, but he knocked the clock from its perch on the mantle and it crashed to the floor, shattering into hundreds of pieces.

The mantle clock glowed brightly, even in daylight.

For a moment, both George and Peter stared at the strange spectacle. Neither saw Gertie standing behind them, raising her arm.

The new husband marveled at the clock in surprise and excitement, as if he were about to say something profound. He reached for the clock, but then his face changed, became tranquil, peaceful. He closed his eyes and fell in a heap on the stone by the fireplace, the hatchet buried deep into the middle of his back. Blood flowed into the narrow channels between the floorboards and striped the floor red all the way to the kitchen.

Gertie stood in horror, her shoulders hunched, her hands over her wordless mouth.

George stood and blinked hard. He nudged Peter's body with his toe and stepped back as if expecting the man to leap to his feet. "Is he dead?"

"It's all over now," Gertie said softly. "He's gone."

"Is he really dead?" George continued softly, "Good."

They both moved to the couch. They sat for ten minutes in silence and without moving.

Finally, Gertie said, "I killed him."

The boy placed his hands on his knees and leaned forward. "You didn't kill him. I did."

Gertie shook her head. "No, Peter."

"Yes, I did. I am going to tell the sheriff. They'll not do much to me because I am just a kid. They'll put you in jail forever if it comes out that you did it."

"Oh, my son. I..."

She let her head fall onto his shoulder and closed her eyes. For a moment, it felt as if nothing had happened, that she and her son were in their house just as they had always been. Just the two of them.

But the dreams had returned. The visions. Visions of him. Her gentle Arthur, the clockmaker. Arthur who gave names to all the calves on their little farm.

George gently stood. He gave Peter's body one more gentle kick. "I am going to the sheriff. It's either you or me, and I won't let you go to jail because of your worthless husband."

Gertie stood beside him and took her son's hand. "What if there were another way?" she asked softly.

He already stood a head taller than she, even though he was only twelve years old. "It's either you or me."

"Go out to the barn for me, please. Get two spades."

"Mother, you're not thinking clearly."

"Go!"

The boy hurried out to the kitchen and outside to the barn. Gertie lifted Peter's legs and spun his body so that his feet were pointed toward the kitchen. She went to the kitchen and got the old throw rug—nobody would miss this old thing. When Peter returned with the spades, they dragged Peter's body through the kitchen to the basement door. They dragged him down the stairs and pulled him past the coal chute to the far corner where the dirt floor was rough and uneven.

George nodded, and Gertie sank her shovel into the loose sand and clay mixture. Wordlessly, they dug a hole six feet long and two wide.

Sweat dripped from Gertie's brow. The work was not unfamiliar.

George's shovel hit something hard, and he leaned down to pull up a rock. He tossed it aside.

Gertie stopped shoveling. She felt a familiar presence filling the dank cellar.

He hit something else that was hard, and he jumped down into the hole and lifted what seemed to be a small tree branch.

"Again?" Gertie heard or possibly said.

In the light that diffused through the narrow basement window, George studied it. It was smooth and gray with knobs on each end. He placed it on the side of the hole and reached down for the next piece, this one round and smooth.

In the dimness, it appeared to be white. His mother stepped silently away from the hole and shook her head slowly.

In the dimness, that round white thing—he touched the jagged edge—a row of human teeth!

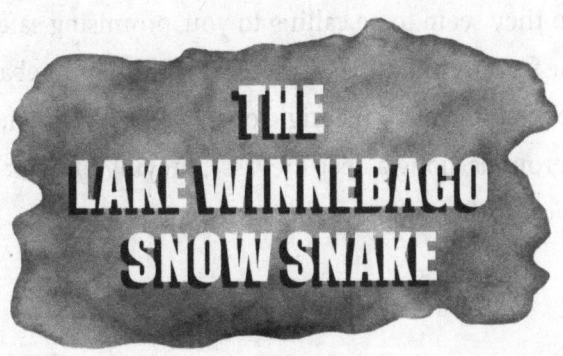

THE LAKE WINNEBAGO SNOW SNAKE

It seems an evolutionary impossibility, but stories persist all across Lake Winnebago of the strange animal that comes out only at night and only in the dead of winter. Snowmobilers cruising the lake heading for the beacon at Lighthouse Point in Neenah or toward Waverly Beach instead are lured into open water by the glowing eyes of the reclusive and predatory Snow Snake, a reptile so secretive that no one has ever photographed one or, indeed, found one alive or dead.

Some say those things that look like eyes are merely optical illusions, hallucinations brought on by cold or too much to drink. Others say they are ghosts of the winter dead searching in the bitter darkness for a safe passage home.

Next time you're out on the frozen lake in the daytime, check along the deserted shoreline for unexplainable holes in the snow and ice, especially along the steep, woody embankments along High Cliff State Park. That is where the snow snakes live and breed.

And if you're unlucky enough to be out on the lake in the dead of a winter's night, don't spend too much time looking out to the open ice. You may see those ghostly red eyes somewhere out there. Do they seem to be calling to you, promising safe passage across the frozen emptiness? Know that it is the Winnebago Snow Snake beckoning you to the frigid open water, luring you to their feeding grounds along a deep crevasse, preying on your fear and desperation as the endless night closes in.

STRAWBERRY GHOST OF HIGH CLIFF

Eric stood, brushed his clothes off, and walked to the water's edge. The setting sun sparkled across the waters of Lake Winnebago as he looked westward across to the factory towns of Neenah and Menasha. The sunset flashed pinks and reds through the billowing clouds of steam and smoke on the far shore. There'd be jobs there, and a long time ago, that would have gotten his attention.

But he hadn't come north for a job.

He held onto a sapling at the water's edge and swung the baited bent nail on a string outward across the water.

He had come north for something very different.

He leaned against the tree and cleared his mind. In the glare of the setting sun, the cork bobber was barely visible. It had been eight weeks since he had seen the green fields of his Missouri home. 1935 had started out passably good—good as anyone can expect, that is, when there's no food, no jobs, no hope—but then came the blackest day of Eric's life, that set him off as a drifter, jumping northward from freight to freight, along dusty, forgotten rights of way. He had a vague idea that if he kept going north, he'd find a place so cold that he'd freeze right through, that his pain would end, that he'd finally make up for what he'd done. A place so cold no flood could find it, no rivers, but ice.

The cork bobbed up and down a few times, but when he checked the hook, except for the drowned worm, there was nothing. Not even a fish would have mercy on him. As his stomach growled empty and hard, as the light in the western sky dimmed like a campfire in the rain, Eric wrapped his blanket closer around his shoulders.

Cold tonight, he thought.

He breathed deeply.

Cold every night.

He leaned his fishing pole against a tree and slung his bag over his shoulder. Who was he kidding, anyway? He didn't know how to fish. He knew how to farm, and not well, at that. And that was about it.

He walked uphill in the twilight, tripping over roots and fallen branches. When one leaf-covered root reached out and grabbed his foot, Eric sank to the ground and curled into a ball. The dirt and leaves smelled just right to him; something that used to be alive and now it decayed back into the stuff that once gave it life. The north wind reached under his collar, chilled his back.

A fearful cold; he cursed his own weakness. He sat up and scanned the forest in the failing light for some kind of shelter, a cave, a spruce, something.

What was that up the hill a ways? A dark shape in the forest, overgrown.

It looked like a boulder from a distance.

He moved closer.

A house. For sure, that is what it was.

A stick snapped underfoot. He crouched in alarm. No good to be caught out at night like this. People get shot for sneaking around, times being what they are.

Closer.

The house, empty.

Forlorn.

And something about it made him sad, as if it had been abandoned by the world, set here to die. Like me, Eric thought. He approached it cautiously. There was no sign of life, no light, no sound.

His feet crunched the newly fallen leaves on the forest floor. He studied the house in the gathering twilight. Moss grew in a thick blanket on the rooftop. The front porch had partially collapsed. A tree had grown through one of the side walls. The wind rose, brought with it the smell of coming snow.

He reached the window of the cabin and peered into the inky black interior.

He could see nothing. If raccoons or, worse, a bear, hadn't found it first, well, maybe Eric had a place for the night. He touched the wooden door frame.

A jolt shot up through his arm and shivered his neck. He jerked his hand away and leaped back. What was that? he wondered. His hand rang with sharp pain as if he had been burned, but he could see no mark on it.

He reached out again, this time cautiously, for the doorknob. He had to find shelter. This was his only chance. When his fingers touched the tarnished brass, he got a similar tingle, but this time much less intense. He pushed against the door, and it swung open.

He stepped across the threshold and into the room. His eyes adjusted to the near-darkness, and he saw a pile of firewood stacked neatly against the fireplace. That was good news, as long as the chimney wasn't blocked. He shuffled slowly across the dirt floor of the cabin and knelt on the slate hearth. He piled up some of the smaller twigs onto the grate and placed a small, split log on top.

He was about to strike a match when the room behind him glowed as if someone had shined a lamp into the room.

He spun fast, held his hand up to protect himself, and stumbled backward.

Then the glow was gone.

He knew he was trespassing, a stranger here, so he'd be at the mercy of whoever owned the place.

Minutes passed, and the light did not return, nor any sound.

He struck the match. The dry kindling caught quickly and sputtered to bright life; flames licked at the log. This would be a good fire, he thought. Too bad he didn't have a nice fish to cook up. At least he'd have a night indoors away from that cold, cold wind.

He rested his hand against the wooden mantel for a moment.

Suddenly, he was knocked backward by the same blast of fear and pain he had felt when he touched the door frame. He tumbled onto his back, landed heavily on the packed dirt floor. Red sparks exploded into the air above him. He covered his eyes.

Too much!

It was all too much!

One night of peace, that's all he needed.

He sat back up. The only light in the room came from the fireplace. All around it on the dirt floor, the glowing kindling was scattered, the embers guttering and dying like starlight at dawn.

For a long time, he sat silent and alert, but nothing more happened.

He exhaled through his teeth. Where could he go, if not here? Where could he sleep, if not here? Probably losing my wits, he thought ruefully. Too much care can break a man.

Outside of the ramshackle cabin, the wind whistled through the trees.

"Please," he whispered. And now it felt to him as if there really were someone else there. "Just one night. Just a little warmth."

He shielded the match as the kindling caught one more time. The bright flame gilded the dry, dead wood. He sat, legs crossed, his arms braced behind him and stared into the fire. Something else was there. Now he was sure of it. It was that same glow as before, coming from just out of sight behind him.

He turned his head slowly, but immediately the light went out again. And when he turned his head back to his fire, fragments of burning wood again had tumbled onto the dirt floor, their bright flame reduced to dying embers.

He felt in his pocket for his matches. Only two left. Well, maybe he didn't really need a fire tonight.

He slid across the dirt floor and leaned his head against the wall. He closed his eyes, too tired to think anymore.

"No fire!" a voice whispered. Small, a girl's voice.

Eric opened his eyes wide, scanned the room. "Who's that?" he hissed.

"No fire. Too much shouting!" the girl's voice said firmly. "My father will be back soon. He's coming."

Eric closed his eyes wearily. Is this how a man loses his mind? He rubbed his forehead. Hungry and cold. Now hearing voices. Too much.

He stood on unsteady legs. "I'll leave the way I came. Thanks for nothing." He walked to the door and pushed against it with his shoulder. Behind him, the strange glow had returned to the room, its faint light spilling out into the darkness. He thought he could feel the air warming behind him, too. He waited.

"My father will be back soon."

"Okay, he'll be back soon. I understand," Eric said gently. "Can I just stay here for a while? It's awful cold out there."

The voice said nothing.

Eric closed the door and sat down heavily with his back to the room. His feet were numb, and his knees creaked stiffly. He saw his faint shadow on the wall in front of him. "What's your name?" he asked.

The small voice giggled. He was happy to hear that sound again. It had been so long. She said, "Silly man. I don't have... Melissa," she said as if surprised to hear herself utter the word. "Melissa is my name."

"That's a fine name. My name's Eric." He coughed once and then many times, struggling to catch his breath. He pulled his thin collar tighter around his neck, but the cold found its way somehow inside.

"Pleased to meet you," she said politely. "Are you from Peshtigo, too?"

"Where?" Eric asked.

"In town, you know," her laughter echoed through the tiny cabin like light and warmth. "I was the Strawberry Princess in 1870. Did you see the parade?"

"No," he said, stunned. 1870. That was over 60 years ago. "No, I've been traveling."

"Are you looking for my father?"

He liked listening to her voice. It was his first real human contact since he left Missouri. "Do you really expect your father home soon?"

"Yes! No. I don't know. I don't know where he went," she said uneasily. "I have been waiting so long."

"You're a good girl to wait for him," he said. He had an idea. He took out the pocket watch his wife had given to him on their wedding day and opened the cover. "I'm sure he'll be back soon." Inside the cover was a mirror. He held it in front of him and aimed it over his shoulder.

In the mirror, he saw the source of the glow.

A girl, maybe 10 years old, in a rocking chair, her hair disheveled, her face stained by dirt and soot. She smoothed the dress across her knees and watched him.

"I like your dress," he said finally.

"My mother—yes—she made it for me. So long ago, I... Her voice trailed off, and the light in the room began to fade.

Eric felt his lonely weeks welling up inside of him. This was the most he had spoken to anyone since the day everything changed. "And you live in Peshtigo?"

"Sure! This is our house."

Eric thought hard for a long time. He knew there was no town anywhere close to here by that name. "I had a daughter about your age."

The girl sniffed. "Had?"

"Mary. She died," Eric said, his voice breaking. "Eight weeks ago. A flood." He cleared his throat. "Her mother, too."

A long silence, but this time, Melissa did not fade.

"That's terrible," she finally said. She chewed on the collar of her dress just like Mary used to. A lump grew in Eric's throat. He studied her face. She continued, "I was in the root cellar pulling some canned strawberries. Mother was making a pie for Saturday dinner. There was a fire..."

"Right here in this cabin?"

"No!" she shouted angrily. "Everywhere! I couldn't find my way home through the smoke. Trees fell all around me, I was burning..." She stood, agitated, and slapped at her legs.

"It's okay, Melissa," Eric said. "You're okay now."

A cold wind whistled through the cabin. Eric shivered. He had wanted to come north, had wanted to freeze his grief in a northern winter, but in the cold darkness he felt something new and alive stirring inside of him.

"I am not okay, and I don't think Father's coming back!" She sobbed, pulling her apron up to dab at her eyes.

Eric watched her through the mirror. He spoke calmly, "All night the men sandbagged downtown. They thought they got ahead of the flood, so they rested after the night's work, cheered the sunrise. They didn't count on the mill dam breaking. Those sandbags, like leaves in the wind. Gone. Just gone." He rubbed his eyes. "Like I said, I wasn't home."

"You were trying to save them. That's a brave thing to do."

Eric snapped, "You think I was there with the rest? I wasn't. I was doing things I shouldn't have been doing. I ran down the hill from her house and watched the whole town tumble down the river, a world of brown water, lumber, trees, dogs, everything. It took me most of the morning to get there against the current. I wasn't even sure I was there once I got there. Nothing left to see." Eric let his head drop. He had been thinking about that day for eight straight weeks, but it was the first time he had spoken out loud about it. "Gone. All gone."

Melissa hesitantly reached out toward Eric's shoulder. "They knew you loved them."

Eric found her face in the mirror. How could he say that he had been a hard man, a drinker, that he really wasn't sure what his family thought of him? The strain of farming, the dull blankness of central Missouri. He ran through the reasons in his mind. Did they know?

In the mirror, Melissa cried silently, miserably. As the golden light dimmed, for a moment, he thought he saw Mary, sad and alone. Eric cleared his dry throat. He had to say something. "I think you would like my little girl. She loved strawberry pie, just like you. Springtime. Late spring. That's the happiest time of year, just the strawberries alone make it so. All kinds of pie she loved. Laughing, singing, dancing. You like to dance?"

Behind him, the room brightened a little bit. In the mirror, he watched Melissa lean closer. "Sometimes I feel like my father is almost home. I can feel him. Hot... The fire! Terrible fire!"

Eric thought hard. A girl, alone, afraid to venture outside, afraid to follow the road out of this meager little cabin. All those decades of loneliness and confusion, waiting for her father to come save her. Eric wiped a tear from his eyes. This little girl, just like his little Mary. Waiting sixty years for her daddy to save her from the fire.

His voice was barely audible even to him. "He misses you. He's been searching for you all this time. Searching for you everywhere. But don't be afraid, Melissa," he whispered. "I'll help you."

Melissa rocked back and forth nervously on her chair. She looked all around the room, as if considering. Finally, she said, "How?"

Eric replied, "Why won't you let me build a fire?"

"It scares me. All the shouting!" She pressed her hands to her ears and sobbed. "It hurts!"

Eric continued reassuringly, "But what did you see when I started the fire?"

"A white light, a tunnel of white light. My father shouting."

"Was he calling to you?"

"He wanted me to stop, to put out the fire. I tried! The smoke! I couldn't find my way home!"

"Hold my hand," Eric said, reaching behind him. In his mirror, he saw her ghostly hand outstretched toward him. It felt as if he had dipped his hand into ice water.

He smiled. He spoke softly, gently, lovingly. "Your father is still trying to find you, Melissa. That's what I think, anyway. I know he'd walk through fire to find you again. I know. I'd walk through fire..."

She clenched his hand tight, and his mind swirled with images from long ago. He saw what she did, knew what she knew. Pain without guilt. The purity of one profoundly wronged.

"Listen to what he is saying this time. Can you do that?"

Melissa squeezed his hand tighter. Eric struck a match against the slate hearth. He held Melissa's cold hand tightly and set the match against the kindling. It flared to life.

Fear pulsed through his hand and down his arm, but still he held on to her tight. Staring into the flame, he, too, saw something strange at the center of it, a glowing white light. Melissa tried to pull away from him, but he held on. "Wait. Do you see that?"

Anguished and terrifying shouts swirled around the cabin. Outside, heavy branches groaned in the rising wind. Flames roared higher in the fireplace, blackening the stone all the way up to the wood mantel and higher. Thuds against the roof, as if rocks rained down from the sky. Yellow flames drew undulating life from the cabin's dry wood. Shouts filled the room, screams of pain and suffering, the roar of an inferno's blast. A terrified jumble, bellowing in agony, voices of hundreds begging for help, burning.

"Make them stop!" Melissa shouted above the din. "Father!" Eric held onto her hand, shielded his eyes from the dizzying swirl of light and sound.

The entire wall in front of him was engulfed in roaring flames that singed Eric's cheeks.

One voice above the roar of the fire, above the agonized shouts of the dying. The soft, sad voice of a father who has lost a child. "Melissa!" the forlorn and broken voice shouted.

The ghostly girl no longer tried to pull away from Eric. Instead, she pulled closer to the fire. "Father?" she whispered. "Father! It's me, I'm here! I'm right here!"

In the glowing white light at the center of the flames, the face of a man, his beard singed by fire, his shirt and face covered in soot. He spun toward them. "Melissa! Is it you?"

"Yes, it's me!" she shouted. "Father!"

A rush of cold, wet wind swept through the cabin as part of the ceiling collapsed. Melissa's hand slipped from Eric's.

The room spun all around him.

He crawled backward toward the door, then he stopped, transfixed.

Inside the fire, Eric saw a little girl in a pretty blue dress bounding across a field of late summer wildflowers toward the bearded man.

The man's face broke into a wide smile as he knelt to embrace his long-lost little girl.

The white light in the fire vanished.

A roof beam crashed to the dirt floor behind him, sending sparks and flames onto his back and his hair. Eric stumbled blindly out into the cold night. Snow and yellow sparks fell as he stumbled through the trees, the fire casting strange ghostly shadows everywhere he looked. Fifty feet from the cabin, he fell to his knees, panting, clothes smoldering, the frigid night air burning his lungs.

The roof of the cabin collapsed in on itself, the fire confined to the antique, dead wood. Snow hissed into the crater and onto his chest. Steam billowed above the dim, orange pile that glowed weakly in the trees. The voices vanished from his mind; the ghostly shadows faded into darkness.

Eric spat on the frozen ground. The soot and smoke had made his mouth taste like death. Soon, sobs of pain and sadness exploded from his chest.

"Mary! I'm sorry!" He clawed at the snow-covered dead leaves on the forest floor. "Eleanor! Forgive me!" He collapsed in pain and numbness to the ground, his blackness complete. He screamed into the earth until his teeth chewed dirt.

Ashes—or snow—fell heavy and silent through the branches, erased memory's rough edge.

He rolled to his back, gritted his teeth, and invited the north inside him like penance.

WE ARE THE STUFF THAT DREAMS

For 72 years, Percy Keene was the stage manager at the Oshkosh Grand Opera House. He died in 1967, but from that date forward, stories continue about a well-dressed old man bustling in the wings during rehearsals, fretting backstage during performances, standing at the back of the house, on the balcony, everywhere a stage manager might be needed. No one really minds when the ghost of Percy Keene shows up—he's an amiable gent, always willing to lend a hand in the cause of good theater.

So, if you're at the Grand one night and you happen to see a man wearing clothes that look out of place, a well-dressed man helping the show run smoothly, give him a smile. That's just the ghost of old Percy Keene getting the old theater up and running for another night of magic.

Now as for the rest of the reports from the Grand— mist rising through the floor, ghost dogs yapping backstage, cold spots, loud laughing in the wings— well, none of it could be real. Could it?

LISTEN TO YOUR MOM

Bruce shielded his eyes from the late October afternoon sun, whose rays slanted in through the windshield. "You *could* use the visor," his mother reminded him.

"I don't want to." He pulled into the lot and put the car in park, then pulled the visor into position. He felt a little foolish doing it, but he wanted to show his mother that he could be trusted with the car once in a while on his own, that he knew what he was doing. And now that he had a job to go with his brand-new driver's license, well, how could his mother argue? He needed a car of his own, even something as antique as his mom's 1999 Maxima would do.

"Make sure you listen to everything your boss says."

"Okay, Mom."

"That's the thing about jobs—you don't get to make decisions on your own. You find out what the boss wants, then you make sure you do it and nothing else." Bruce silently undid his seatbelt. "You got that?"

"Yes." All Bruce could see in the window of Elysian Self Storage was the reflection of his mother's car in the bright sunshine looking a little beat up all of a sudden. Used to be Bruce's father's car all those years ago. She probably never meant to keep it so long, but when the person with the good job in the family dies, the other people make do with what he leaves behind. So, they pushed this car as far as it would go. Only the two of them. How long would it last? With money so tight, Bruce didn't want to follow that though through to its logical outcome.

The man on the phone—Mr. Virgil—sounded nice, so Bruce wasn't too concerned. And it wasn't like it was his first real job or anything. The summer before, he had worked as a substitute ice cream man. And he sold balloons at the Fox River Mall, too, but only for maybe half a day. But that was a story for another day.

"Anyway, I know you'll do well. Look at me." She licked his finger and rubbed Bruce's face around his lips. He pulled away spasmodically, wiping his mouth with his sleeve.

"Stop it! Come on, that's just gross!"

"Okay, but it won't be my fault if you show up for work one day with peanut butter smeared across your cheeks." Then she smiled. "Go knock 'em dead. I'll pick you up in the morning. Seven good?"

Bruce opened the door and got out. He checked himself out in the plate-glass window. He looked small and crooked, half in shadow and half in bright light. He tried to dress for the night, but what does one wear to a job that has no contact at all with any other person? Medium height, medium build, sandy brown hair, okay face: all averageness, as far as Bruce's eyes could see. Looking around, the building was in good shape, like most in Rosemont.

Clean parking lot, new-looking masonry all around. Even out here on the highway, in the rough side of town, the storage places were nicer than the churches in Campbelltown. Bruce held his breath, took the first step toward the door.

His mother cranked down the driver's-side window. "Don't forget your dinner or lunch or whatever it is." She handed him the white plastic bag she filled with enough sandwiches and snacks for a polar expedition. Bruce sheepishly took it, mumbled thanks. In the distance, he heard church bells.

Inside the office, his eyes needed a couple of seconds to adjust. The interior office was dark, but clean, well-maintained. The silence made the place seem more like a church than a place where people stored the junk their garages wouldn't hold. He stood at the counter, which stretched to the walls covered by old posters of nature scenes hung, some of them limply, from tacks stuck into the walls. The place had an air of disuse, although it was clean. Somewhere behind the counter, a door opened and closed. True, he was nervous; this job was important, maybe the start of something big. From out of the shadows, Mr. Virgil stepped into the office. He was youngish, maybe in his early thirties, well-dressed, as if he were at a party on a yacht rather than working at a grungy self-storage place and strode confidently up to Bruce and extended a hand. "Glad to meet you, Bruce. I see you found the place okay."

Bruce stepped back and returned the greeting; glad his voice didn't crack. They spoke for a bit, mostly Mr. Virgil asking Bruce questions about his school and home life. Sure, his new boss was the young Republican type—free market this and private property that—but he had an energy about him, a charisma, that Bruce found engaging. They stepped outside to look around the place. Mr. Virgil spoke as if the place were his life's work, the greatest storage place in America. "Here's Building One. You'll see that we've got two buildings here separated by the driveway over here. One is bigger than Two by a little bit." He pointed out that both were two stories tall, and that they were laid out in L's that almost nested into one another. "These," Mr. Virgil pointed at the one-car garage doors that lined the outer first floor of both buildings, "and the interior rooms hold all manner of our constituents' surplus. Some of these outer chambers have cars in them, just about all of them are occupied. See, once people find objects, they love but have no use for, they need an extra room. That's where we come in."

Mr. Virgil stood with his hands on his hips, beamed proudly as he spoke. He put his hand on Bruce's shoulder, "Tonight, you are to do three things. First, you pay attention. Someone comes in and wants a room, get their info and tell them I'll call them in the morning. At eight-thirty, you walk the yard and tell anyone you meet that we're closing at nine sharp and they need to get out. At nine, you lock the gate. The lights in the yard are on a timer. No need to walk the grounds after nine. Stay in the office and monitor the cameras. Call me if anything unusual happens. Don't call the police. It's usually something I can handle easily. At midnight, a man should drop off the dogs; they should sniff around and make a racket if anyone does anything, and they should be gone before sunrise. So, all you have to do is make sure everyone is out by nine, then watch these monitors.

"And it goes without saying that you don't touch anyone's things. That's rule number one." Bruce nodded and tried to look serious.

Five minutes later, Mr. Virgil was gone.

Bruce sat alone in the office and watched dust dance in the thin shaft of light that knifed in through the back door. Slowly, sunset stole that diversion. Bruce poked through the rental agreements and new constituent information packages that lay in folders on top of the file cabinet. Inside the top drawer were a dozen combination padlocks. They all said "The Classic" on them and had red faces with white numbers from 1-39. The loop of steel was likewise painted red. The single sheet of paper in the drawer had the numbers 37-6-3 and the letters RLR written on it. The combination? But for which one? He tried the first lock. It opened immediately. The second one, as well. The third, fourth, all of them that same combination and none other. Maybe some customers needed a lock. Not a bad item to have on hand in a place like this. Probably could make a killing on the markup. But all the same combination?

A large, hard-cover notebook—an accounting ledger—that had begun to yellow with age sat inside the second drawer. The many pages appeared to record everyone who had ever rented one of the storage rooms. There were dozens of entries on each page, but in the light pencil scratches, he could make out a single number or letter here or there, but nothing like a complete word. In the column where he expected to see the dates, he saw numbers like 1923 and 1977, so maybe they weren't dates after all. Bruce laughed—imagine paying for a room to store the junk of previous generations! Those must be some irreplaceable yet completely unnecessary items! Deeper into the book, the pages were stiff with age, as if they had not been separated in many years. Strange.

Studying the ledger, he didn't notice the shadow outside, the hand on the door, the slow, steady force that opened it behind him. Bruce turned a page, tried to make out the faint handwriting, still with no luck.

Silent footsteps crossed the linoleum, stopped directly behind Bruce. A hand, reaching, the young man, oblivious. The hand touched his shoulder! A scream!

"Aagghhh!" Bruce spun too quickly, dropped the book to the floor. A brown-haired young woman smiled through the pink bubble she clenched in her lips. "Renee! I almost had a heart attack."

"Serves you right! What kind of security guard are you, anyway?"

Bruce picked up the book and tried unsuccessfully to wedge it back into the drawer. "I'm not a security guard, okay? Assistant Property Manager. Where'd you come from?" Renee had no car, and Rosemont was a few miles down the highway.

"George dropped me off after work. I think he likes me!" She boosted herself up on the counter, searched with her face for his, lips ready to kiss.

"Stop it!" Bruce snapped. "What if a customer walks in and I'm all lovey-dovey with you?" Renee looked back into the empty parking lot. She started to laugh. And finally, Bruce joined her. "You know I need a career. Any real girlfriend would be more supportive."

"Career?" Renee gestured around the office but then sagged when she saw the hurt in Bruce's eyes. "Okay, all kidding aside. I'm proud of you for getting this job. I'm already figuring out how I'm going to spend your paycheck, you know." That made him smile. They were mismatched, always had been. Bruce was known as the steady, straight kid. A good student, honest, hard-working. Renee was the party girl. Sure, she got decent grades, too, but if there were good times to be had, Renee was in the middle of it. Their friends were shocked when they "came out" that day at lunch. They demanded a public kiss to "prove" they were a couple. But they were together now for longer than anyone, including themselves, had expected.

He turned back to the drawer. "Can you help me with this?" Bruce had gotten the book halfway into the drawer, but no further. "Just help me get it back into the drawer, okay?"

Renee took the book out of the drawer, spun it once, flipped it, and slid it easily back inside the drawer, exactly as he had found it. Bruce grumbled. She reached around and grabbed his bottom. "You know, I'm pretty good at slipping big things into tight places."

"Please stop that." How had she gotten those books into the drawer so easily? "You know I don't like it, why do you do it?"

"Because I love you, you dork. And you don't know a good thing when it's spread out naked on the floor at your feet." Bruce scooped up Mr. Virgil's phone, walked past the counter and out the front door. Renee followed him. "I'm sorry!" she said. That was their routine. Bruce walked behind the office building, a low one-story house with a garage attached. He held out his hand as he walked. Renee fell into step next to him, her hand curling warmly into his.

"You don't have to say sorry." That was their routine, too. Kind of like foreplay, except they had not yet had sex, not that Renee hadn't tried pretty much every day since she met him. Thanks for the help with those books. I really couldn't figure it out."

"You're welcome." They walked, her head on his shoulder, to the driveway between the buildings. The sun had gone down, the air had cooled considerably. Bruce saw no one working at their storage room, saw no cars or U-Hauls rolling in or out of the gate lately. By his reckoning, the place was empty. And it was almost eight. Another hour, and he could settle in for the night with his books and the music on his iPod. And if Renee stuck around, they could just talk. Not bad for the first day at a new job. "So, what's in these big buildings?"

"Seems like just a lot of junk, if you ask me. These rich people have huge houses and still they buy more and more until they can't even fit it in their house." Bruce reached for the back door of Building One. He gave it a tug and for a moment, it opened. Then it was as if someone grabbed it from the other side and pulled back. It slammed shut. Bruce stumbled backward; Renee caught him.

"Open a door much?" She laughed. Bruce stood again, reached for the door, and carefully opened it. The door squeaked against its steel frame, but it opened smoothly. Strange, Bruce thought. They entered the long hallway, endless rows of locked doors on either side of them, a dim intersection in the distance. "Too weird!" Renee ran ahead, punching at doors, counting out "One, two, three, four!" as she banged along the corridor. Bruce was glad Mr. Virgil was not here to see this. He ran after Renee and grabbed her by the arm.

"Please stop that!" Renee jerked her arm away and yelled again, running down the hall banging on each door.

"Why should I? That's the problem with you—no sense of when to make a racket!" Bruce followed behind her. He walked stiffly, again, embarrassed by Renee. This was also their routine. She stopped at the end of the hall where the doors became less frequent. "These must be bigger rooms inside. I bet one of these is bigger than my apartment! If only we could get inside it, look around. Maybe there's gold or diamonds or drugs or something we could use..."

"You can't steal from these people. Besides, they're all locked." Bruce put his hand on the lock at the door. Familiar. Red outline, the word "The Classic" engraved into the red metal. Same as the locks in the file cabinet. When Renee wandered off around the corner, Bruce played with the lock. What were those numbers? He tried a few combinations of 6 and 3 and 37. Or was it 36 and 18 or something?

Engrossed as he was, he did not notice the door behind him move. At first, it seemed to be a trick of the light. Then, almost imperceptibly, the steel door creaked open inch by inch. Darkness within revealed no force by which the door moved. No hand could be seen.

An inch, then two, then a foot.

Had he turned, he might have seen a hand, pale, thin, pushing steadily outward. But Bruce heard nothing. He spun the tumbler: 37-6-3, pulled the lock toward his waist. To his surprise, it snapped open! He looked up and down the hallway for Renee, but she was gone. Just as well. She probably would just want to rip the place up, go through everything. Bruce pulled the door wide open and stood staring into the dimness.

"Renee!" he called. Louder a second time. No answer.

The room was filled to the edge with plain cardboard boxes of all shapes and sizes, all neatly stacked. He touched the boxes, felt their density, their great mass, as if they were filled with sand or metal. Suddenly, two cold, thin hands covered Bruce's eyes.

"Boo!" Renee whispered in his ear. Bruce jumped, spun, dropped the lock. The door across the hall slid closed as silently as it had opened. Renee flipped the timer switch on the wall next to the door.

"Agh! Don't ever do that again!" They both looked down to see him grasping her wrist tight, too tight.

"Let go, please." Bruce dropped her wrist, muttered "sorry" and turned to close the door. "Who left this one open?" She pushed past him and touched the boxes as far up as she could reach. "What's all this? Any idea?"

"No. And we don't belong here playing around with this stuff."

She opened one of the boxes and took out a small stack of photos. "I mean, look at these people! They came and went in a blink, and who cared? They probably hated Black people and worked until they died." She dropped the photos to the floor. "And look at this thing!" She held up an antique scythe. "So, these farmers loved their short, miserable lives so much that they passed their lawn mowers down to their grandchildren who then keep it all locked up here? Can't you see how insanely stupid it all is?"

She opened another box and pulled out a long, white dress. "Somebody got married—or not! Look!" She held up a price tag still tied by a small string to the sleeve. "That's a country song, right there!" She dropped the dress to the floor, and, at that moment, the main hallway lights went out leaving only the emergency lights at each end of the hallway to illuminate the place. Must be the timer, he thought. He waited for his eyes to adjust to the near darkness.

He took her by the shoulder and gently spun her away from the room. He closed the door, relatched the handle, and slid the padlock into its hook. He closed the lock and spun the tumblers.

Renee's eyes widened. "You did it! How did you know the combination?"

"I did not open it. It was open. I am just closing it."

Renee stepped back. "Are you lying to me, Bruce? I told you that you can do anything you want, as long as you never, ever lie to me." Bruce stood with the lock in his hand, staring at it. He said nothing. "I don't want anything to do with a liar. I told you I've had way too much of that bullshit in my life already." She turned and walked away.

"Wait. Okay." Bruce caught up to her. "I just don't want you messing around in here, that's all." He pointed at the nearest lock. "See that one? And that one? And that one over there? I think I can open all of them."

She pulled him close, her hands in his back pockets, her fingers flexing. "Show me, please? Just one more? I only want to see what's so important that these rich people can't do without."

Bruce had no resistance to her smile. He opened another door.

The inside of this was very different from the first room they had seen. For one thing, they could see all the way in. In one corner was a low pile of mattresses. Along one wall sat a long table covered in books of all shapes and sizes. The floor was mostly open space, the hallway light angling across its dust-covered surface.

Renee slipped past Bruce and danced across the room. She jumped on the mattresses and rolled to her side, propped on one elbow, patted the mattress next to her, and winked. "Come on over here, you handsome man." She lay on her back with her knees up, legs parted. "I have a little storage room with your name on it!"

Bruce rolled his eyes. "Come on, Renee. Why do you always have to do this?"

"Bruce!" Renee's eyes opened wide, surprise and shock in her face. "Come over here, quick!" Bruce walked carefully over to her. When he got next to the bed, she laughed, pulled him on top of her, hugged him tight with her arms and legs. Bruce struggled, but they stopped.

"It's like you want me to get fired or something. Why can't you just be a normal person once in a while?"

"Normal people have sex, Bruce. You're the one who is abnormal. I swear, I don't know why I spend time with you. You're such a prude." It was the way their conversations frequently went. This time, Bruce did not move. He lay on top of her, thinking. Maybe she was right. Maybe I was the one with the problem. But if they had sex every time she wanted to, they'd never get the chance to put clothes on. Bruce started laughing at the thought of constant copulation, the calories they'd burn, all the fluids they'd need to drink.

"Okay, you win," she said as she walked out in a cloud of dusty anger.

Bruce lay there, head cradled by an arm, heard the fire door open and shut, the sound of her footsteps diminishing into silence. Another messed-up little love session for Renee and Bruce. She's so friendly, Bruce thought, but she's not a good listener. Why can't I ever have a say in what we do or where we go? It seemed to him that she had a fixed set of ideas, what was right, what she wanted, and if Bruce didn't conform to that, well, then she would be finished with him. But she could be flexible. She was often patient with him, tried to rein herself in, especially in public, especially with his family. Somewhere behind his head, he heard a scrape of metal against metal, as if a stuck door were opening.

"Renee!" No answer.

He shouted again louder.

Nothing.

He got up and sat at the edge of the pile of mattresses. The scraping didn't sound like a fire door. It seemed like it came from somewhere inside the wall. He walked to the hallway. No one was there. He closed and locked the door to the mattress room and walked in the direction Renee had gone.

He passed through the first fire door.

Still no sign of her.

At the four-way intersection, still no sign of her.

"Renee!" he shouted.

He heard a far-off door slam. Maybe she was playing a game now, her silence saying, "Come find me!" Bruce trotted after the sound, opened a door ahead. Stairs led upward to the second floor. Above him, he heard a loud squeak, then a slam.

Another door.

But he was getting closer. He could feel it.

At the top of the stairs, he pushed through the door and scanned the hallways. To his left, a fire door was just swinging shut.

He ran down that hall, excited for the chase, the blood flowing through his body and his mind—maybe that room with the mattresses would see some action yet tonight! He pushed his way through the fire door to find himself at a four-way intersection. He thought he heard a sound to his right, and he ran after it, winding his way around corners, pushing his way through one fire door after another.

Finally, he stopped to listen.

Silence.

Mostly.

No running footsteps, but again, that same light scraping coming from somewhere beyond the door in front of him.

He pressed his ear to the door, but the sound neither faded nor grew louder.

The lock, a Classic, the same red one he knew. With no one in sight up and down the hallway, he spun the wheel, let it fall at 37-6-3.

The lock opened in his hand.

Inside, a thin, pale figure stood silent and still; a man, small, underfed, fraying brown tweed blazer, his head wrapped in a scarf, his entire appearance antique, as if he had stepped out of a history book. His skeletal hands opened and closed at his sides, as if unused to movement.

Bruce took a slow half-step backward when the man lunged at him. All at once, strong arms gripped him, and Bruce was dragged into the storage room. He wanted to scream, but the pressure was simply too much. Darkness spun around him, as if he had been devoured by some ravenous beast. The arms threw him forward into the room where he tumbled headlong into the darkness and smashed his head against something edgy and hard.

He came to rest face down on something soft.

Something soft and bony.

He felt an arm and then shoulders.

He pressed into something sticky and wet and lifted himself up and off.

In the dimness, a person in a gray dress. Or was it white?

Behind him, the door slammed shut.

Renee's shoulders, her hands: he'd know them anywhere.

Outside, the scrape of metal against metal and click of a lock being reattached to the door.

He pushed himself to his knees. Renee's body, yes, dressed in white. She was all there—except that her head was gone!

CAN'T FIND A BETTER MAN

Melissa fingers the neck of the guitar like it's a fragile animal, picks at the wide-open power chords, wahs her way through scales up and down the fretboard, dances on the foot switches, trying to find the sound he made, that shimmering fire he seduced nightly from the thin neck of the Gibson ES-355, the Fender Twin Reverb.

Melissa practices to forget about Joey.

She practices to remember him.

The words scrawled on a yellow legal pad, the chords in block letters along the side, she sings:

> I'll find a way
>
> to make him feel much better
>
> I'll find a way
>
> to keep the night from his eyes
>
> though he's away
>
> I'll write it down in this letter
>
> I'll find a way

There's got to be a way

And she believes there is a way to make it all better.

Sometimes when she's playing, she feels heat coming off the strings, intense, breath-stealing, lung-burning heat, like the night out at the crossroads north of Appleton, when Pearl Jam serenaded both of them: Joey's cremation and Melissa's broken leg twisted under her in the watery ditch, the guitar case beside her. She tried, but she couldn't get close enough to see if he died by impact or by the flames.

And now she practices all the time with the ferocity of a woman driven by necessity. She believes in wishes, you see, and she wishes hard, lets the music pull from the air the immaterial, to make it alive, breathing. She believes in wishes, believes that time can be wound back up again.

And so, she practices.

The crowd at Waterfest surges toward the stage as the guitarist steps to them, her silver sequins flashing in the stage lights, her blonde hair falling like aurora borealis across the night sky of her black leather back, silver stud leather belt, and faded blue jeans. Her band started out slow that night—ballads, love songs—to get the crowd to smolder, but now, well past midnight, the fifth and final band of the night, they get down and dirty, give the audience what it came for, crank their amps to distort, scream into the mics, let the savagery of rock and roll flow like sweat off their bodies, through their clothes, and into the air until the night is thick with it: the ghosts of everything that lives and dies and has regrets about chances not taken, lost love, and death coming too soon, too soon, whirl in the air above the dance floor. The whole world catches fire, and the band pours blistering heat from the stage right back at them. The music soars higher and higher, while the dirt dance floor rumbles. No one wants anything other than to be in the music, to soar with the band, to fly to the sky, and never to come back down.

Melissa kicks out from the front of the stage, her fingers dancing along the neck of the Gibson. She marvels at her hands as they blur in modes and scales, she only vaguely imagines. This is it, she thinks. This song—and where did it come from? The jangling guitar roars out of her amp, the climbing, soaring chords of "She Believes," every verse an electric touch, every chorus a climax:

> She's young, but there's a sadness
>
> hidden in that pretty face.
>
> She lights a candle and cries,
>
> holds a picture of her lover who has died,
>
> she believes in wishes and the candle burns,
>
> in the wrecked car her lover burned,
>
> she believes in wishes, she wishes hard,
>
> She holds her hand above the flame,
>
> feels what he felt, hears,
>
> "You make me crazy girl. I still love you, girl."

She blinks at tears,

the wish takes hold,

She believes she believes she believes,

and!

(the crowd shouts these words in unison, eyes clenched shut, fists raised, like a prayer)

and she!

(a growl of regret and passion, throw it all away to find one true thing in this world)

and she burns!

(arms raised in victory over everything anyone had ever known)

The song changes—modulates up a step, tempo kicks up, too, as the band rushes headlong into the bridge where waves of bass, piano, guitar, and cymbals crash along the shore of the audience, soaking them in the anguish of lost love. Melissa raises her eyes to the black sky and smiles, open-mouthed, gasping in happiness like a little child. She turns to her band and nods to each of them, holding out the guitar as her fingers slide along the neck, her hips swing back and forth with the beat, the happiest the band has ever seen her. Sweat shines on her cheeks in the stage lights' glare. "Thank you!" she mouths to her bandmates. They, too, are caught up in the night, the explosion of the boundary between here and some other where.

Above the drums, the held fifth, the bass throbs on the root, Melissa turns to the crowd and shouts, "Who's burning with me?" And all the men in the crowd, and the women too, shout "Yeah!" and let themselves be carried by the swirling chords, the distorted jangle of the guitar, a sound they had never heard in their lives, a sound they didn't think possible.

The guy at the light board must have felt it, too, because he made the stage sparkle like the beginning of the universe, bright lights and blankness fighting for control, dancing a hard grind right out there in the middle of the dance floor with everyone else.

And for a long time, the band played that progression, letting it roll out before them like the wide-open plains, the speed along the runway, taking flight, lifting into the sky. Melissa holds the D chord against the progression, lets it jangle for a measure, then two and more, turns to the band and raises her arm. "This is it," she shouts above the roar of bass, drums, and guitar. "This is it!" She leans forward, feet splayed wide under her, banging away at that D chord, her head hanging low nearly touching the stage in front of her. The band holds the note along with her now—the crowd shouts for more, poised on the knife edge between exhaustion and elation—

Then something strange.

The band...

—trips somehow

as if for a moment, time stops

the strobe holds steady, blinds everyone

in the echoing silence

the last cymbal crash reverberates from the walls

the dancers hang suspended between beats—

A thunderous snare beat drops from the sky and the song picks up again, modulated up one more step, the tempo kicked higher. The singer growls into the mic, his arms glisten with sweat against his black tee shirt, his fingers rolling like electric current along the neck:

I light a candle, play my guitar

there's the picture of my lover who has died

The band behind him bounces along with the beat, lost in the music.

Something has happened to the crowd, too. They've gone past dancing to something else. They each, in their own space, shake to the music as if possessed by spirits of the long and angry dead. The jangling guitar finds a softer edge and washes over them like a flood of clear, cool water. Love, fear, shyness, inhibition: the jangling guitar washes over everyone, cleanses everything.

She was young, but there was a sadness

hidden in that pretty face.

And Joey brings them down from the song's climax, as he's done before, presses down against the air with his hands, but the band doesn't need telling. They've already been to that mountaintop. And climbed back down. Soon, it's just Joey and muted, picked notes on his Gibson, a soft calliope with a gentle barker, inviting you inside to see wonders you never imagined:

The candle burns, calls to me,

my hands are too cold to play.

I don't believe, don't believe, don't believe

in wishes, no, not today.

Joey holds the final chord—the shimmering suspended D—reverbed and delayed—and lets it sustain until no one is sure whether the sound comes from the guitar or from inside themselves.

The crowd roars its approval, and the band stands arm in arm at the front of the stage. They bow and let it soak into them. Tim squeezes Joey's shoulder and shouts into his ear, "You made us tonight, man!"

Joey looks around the room and feels something, somehow, wrong, different about tonight.

He looks across the stage at his three best friends and rubs his eyes. For a moment, he is dizzy, grabs the mic stand to steady himself. Somebody's missing, he thinks. He tries to remember who it could be, but everything he remembers leads him to this place, this moment, with his friends, the conquerors, the rock and roll stars in this little northern outpost.

But the feeling remains, shakes through him like a passing freight. Tim, Slug, Westie, and... He opens his eyes again. They had aged since when? This afternoon? Nothing makes sense, he thinks.

Without her, nothing makes sense.

Melissa.

Dead these three years.

She's missing.

The mic next to his, Exene and John, Nico and Lou, Merry and Mick, Stevie and TP. All of it, everything, gone.

The crowd sings the final verse of that song they just ripped through. They sing it again, those words—the pronouns are wrong. How did they—?

He scans the crowd—a woman, her back to him, in a black leather jacket making her way toward the parking lot, leaving the scene. Blonde hair falls in curls down her black leather back, the curves of her body, the tight, faded blue jeans.

Joey leaps from the stage, knocks a mic stand down—his band mates say, "Hey!" but he's gone, into the crowd, following that woman, the one who made him want to shout, "Melissa!"

There she is, in the parking lot, getting into a car, the driver's side, the door shuts. Joey at her window—rain splattered, wipes it clear—she opens the window a crack—their eyes meet— Joey apologizes—not who he thought she was—she looks disappointed—he smiles and stumbles back across the parking lot.

What did he expect?

Much later that night, Tim finds Joey crouched against the outside of the building. "I'm not supposed to be here," Joey mutters, wipes his eyes.

Tim touches his shoulder. "No one is supposed to be at Cranky Pat's," he laughs.

"I'm not supposed to be here," Joey says and waves his hand out toward Commercial Street, toward the rest of Neenah, the whole universe.

That night, Joey dreams of Melissa. She is happy, touching him, making him laugh. They play "Love Me Do" and then they do.

In his dreams.

He wakes up in the apartment he shares with the band and sits by the window all day strumming the unplugged Gibson. The hollow body of the Electric Spanish hums against his hip. He tries to find the sound he heard for just a moment in the air that night at Cranky Pat's. A D chord it was, but not down low on the neck—a different kind of D—the strings felt soft in his hands that night, like fingers touching him back. All day he sits and looks for that chord. It's right there on the neck someplace.

Right there.

Just out of reach.

Like some ghost.

A week passes, and the band plays Waverly Beach. They start the song "She Believes," and Joey bounces along with the chord changes, his mind wandering back to the night and the woman in black leather—the woman who looked so much like Melissa. He searches the crowd for her again—he isn't sure why—he feels protective of her somehow, as if she should be there, as if she should be there to find him.

The Gibson is a guitar in his hands that night, nothing more. A nice guitar, but that's all.

But what should it be? Joey wonders. That's all it can be, right?

The song ends, their show ends, and that's that. His band looks at him kind of funny as they pack their gear. "You were someplace else tonight, man," Tim says.

Joey smiles. "Thanks for picking me up. You guys sounded great," he said. And meant it.

He practiced all week—where was that chord, that sound? —the overtone of the fifth, the purity of a unison someplace, a suspension somewhere, too.

He just couldn't find it.

His band saw the change in him. All the practice made his playing transcendent. His guitar shimmered like the rising moon on the ocean. He led the band with the ferocity of a man driven by necessity. Music wasn't just a good time anymore. He didn't say a word about it, but they knew: he was looking for something that he just couldn't find.

Many years later, Joey's band winds up a show at The Elbow Room. They play "She Believes," the good old song that the crowds used to know, but now it bounces off the dark wood-paneled walls like any other thump in the raucous bar. Joey knows the guys he's playing with now no way, no how compare to his old friends who quit the scene to raise families.

But not Joey.

He still plays the progression like he always does, places every D he knows against the beat crosswise, slotted in, upbeat, and downbeat. He barely lifts his eyes to see who's listening anymore.

At closing time, a surprise: His old friend Tim waves to him from the bar. "Joey! How's the rock star life?" They walk to the corner of the room where the band is breaking down their gear.

Joey smiles, exhausted. He blows air out from his cheeks. "Still getting after it."

Tim puts his hand on Joey's shoulder. "I'm worried about you, man. You need a break." Tim smiles and laughs, but Joey knows from his eyes that Tim is serious. "You look horrible."

Joey hefts his guitar case, nods to his younger bandmates. The rest of the gear is theirs. "I'll see you fellas."

They wave, coil wires.

"Can I buy you a beer?" Tim asks.

Joey looks around the small room, takes a deep breath. "I gotta go, Tim. I gotta practice."

He leaves his old friend standing at the bar, his arm outstretched to clasp his. Joey walks away, his eyes half closed.

If he could just find that chord, that sound, he could bring her back. He knows it, has known it ever since that night at Waterfest all those years ago when the whole world slipped away.

Melissa.

In his dreams, the song on the radio when they crashed was Pearl Jam, "Better Man."

She can't find a better man.

And the shame of it is the song's right, he thinks.

The song is right.

THE UNLUCKY GROOM

Valley Road in Menasha is the place where the most embarrassed ghost in the Fox Cities haunts.

He dressed in his finest Sunday clothes: long coat, shirt, collar, and tie. He was a man known for his fastidiousness, and even on weekends he was still the best-dressed man in Menasha. He took special care on this important day, especially with his tie. In fact, on this day, he spent so much time getting his outfit perfect that when he finally glanced up at the clock, he realized he was late for his own wedding! He rushed out the door. How could it be that a man known for such attention to detail could be late on this momentous day? He urged his old horse east on Valley Road. He was bound for Appleton Road, for the church where he'd meet his love, and they'd begin their lives together. Well, he pushed his poor horse a little too hard, a little too fast, and that old nag got a little squirrely, caught a wagon wheel in a rut, and drove herself and that young man straight into the tree-lined ditch along the side of the road. Well, this young man saw it coming, and he stood up in the cart and tried to jump off before the whole thing crashed down into the mud. Luckily, the groom grabbed onto a thin overhanging tree limb, but it wouldn't support his weight. When the branch broke, he spun through the air in such a way that he flew backward into the trunk of the tree with a thud. But strangely, he didn't fall. Something had him by the back of the neck. He squirmed silently, unable to breathe, and found that the loop of his tie, so neatly and tightly knotted, had caught onto the stub of the broken branch that protruded from the trunk of the tree. He tried to work his fingers into the knot, but the weight of his body pulled the silk far too tight. Breathlessly, he cursed the worthless horse that had spooked and run off, dragging the broken cart behind her. There the groom hung, his voice choked out of him, obscured from the road by the thick vegetation, his legs flailing at the air, finding nothing even remotely strong enough to support his weight. Slowly, as the sun climbed into the sky on his wedding day, the groom lost consciousness and soon died.

The bride's family found his body later that day after a loud search involving muskets and axe handles. Some thought he had killed himself, but no one could square that idea with how they had found him, hanging there with his feet only inches from the ground. If only his tie had a little bit of slack in it, he might have been able to squeeze out of it. If only...

A bizarre accident, that's what they told the heartbroken bride-to-be. The wedding feast became the groom's funeral dinner.

To this day, travelers along Valley Road on early Sunday mornings report meeting a confused young man dressed from a time long past, hoarsely whispering that he is late for his own wedding, and would they please, please, please, please help him get to the church on time?

THE GREENVILLE WATERWITCH

Jack rested his head against the dusty pane of the coach door. Flat land rattled by as the stage bumped and bounced along the pitted and rutted twin track that led west out of Appleton into farmland and forest. He sat back in his chair and read the newspaper advertisement once again:

Don't waste time Digging Dirt—

I'll find a Well for you Lickety Switch—

Water Witch for Hire—

Erastus Munger, Greenville, Wisconsin

The size of the ad alone made it stand out. Plenty of people called themselves water witches or dowsers or whatever, but most of them were local people with the "gift" who made a little bit of money from their neighbors and families. But this man Munger had money enough for a quarter-page ad in the *Crescent* and confidence enough in his abilities to spread his name far and wide. That marked him as different.

Jack looked down at his hands. The once-familiar brown spots had returned to mar the youthful lines of his strong fingers. He had grown accustomed to the back of his hand the way it used to be, the smooth skin, the dark hair. He loved being young again after so long. In only a few months, he had worked his way back up to foreman at the Vulcan Mill. No one knew what became of the grumpy old man who used to work there, and Jack was chagrined to find out that very few cared either way.

Nor did the man in black return, although Jack listened for the lonely wail of a train whistle late in the night.

He could feel it coming when the spirit weakened. Could feel his body aging a few years every day. And he knew what he had to do to save himself.

This time, he knew it when he started having trouble getting out of bed in the morning. The flesh started to sag on his upper arms and his gut. He didn't like the feeling, not one bit. He started to look around for signs.

Jack had a feeling about this water witch, a feeling that something wasn't right.

The coach stopped in front of the Green Bay and Lake Pepin rail depot. Jack hopped to the ground stiffly. The breeze had kicked up since he left Appleton, and a heavy, dark bank of clouds roiled to the west. The town was small enough so that Erastus Munger's sign stood out. It was huge and painted blue, saying " Waterwitching Done Here." Had to be the place.

Jack knocked at the front door. No answer. He tried the handle, and the door swung inward. The office was clean and empty. Only a small table stood in the center of the room on which a map of the area had been spread. Penciled onto the map were small x's, likely where this dowser had done his work in the past. On a small piece of paper that rested on top of the map, Jack saw today's date—June 9, 1909—and this: "Old Gray Farm House just past the Church." The hand shook that wrote it, as if the writer was old and feeble. Dowsing's a hard life for an old-timer. He'd be doing him a favor.

Jack let his fingers glide lightly along the tabletop as he walked to the far end of the room and a thick, wooden door. He touched the wood with his fingertips as if he expected it to be hot. Then he knocked, softly at first, then loudly. He tried the handle, and the door opened up to reveal a richly decorated living room filled with paintings and fine furniture. A huge wooden cabinet along the far wall was filled with books and carved figures of animals and nature scenes. Jack whistled softly. This dowser's possessions must be worth a small fortune.

He closed his eyes and listened intently.

Nothing.

The outer door latch clicked behind him.

Jack silently swung the inner door shut and turned to see a young man coming in out of the gray afternoon. The young man coughed, tried to hold back the next one, and ended up doubled over in pain as the coughing spasm rolled through his body. As he bent at the waist, a thick leather bag that hung on his back swung forward and nearly touched the ground. The young man recovered, slung the bag back behind his back, and wiped his mouth.

Jack cleared his throat, and the young man jumped. "I've got a well that needs digging," Jack lied.

The young man smoothed out his vest and grunted.

"Wanted to maybe watch how you work, learn a little bit, so I don't waste my money on a fake."

The young man frowned at Jack. "A fake, eh?" Then a smile slowly crept across his face. "I'm the best there's ever been. I'm on my way now—you can come along if you like."

As Munger shuffled the papers on his desk, Jack casually walked to his side and let his hand dangle near the bag. The faint, familiar feeling of dread and fear washed over him. A tingle ran up Jack's arm. He recoiled, glad for the darkness of the office so Munger couldn't see the surprise on his face. That was it! The source of his success, part of the ghostly shipment from Peshtigo all those months ago at Vulcan, timber that had been milled and shipped all over, used in every kind of different thing a man can make out of wood.

Now, in his mind, Jack heard the familiar and distant voices of agony and terror, one voice among others, a young girl's, shouting something unintelligible.

But just as he was about to grab the bag, to reach inside, to place his hands on the wood itself, to absorb its energy, Munger slung it over his shoulder. The ghostly girl's anguished voice faded. Munger walked to the door, saying, "We've got to hurry."

"Wait, I—" Jack said, but it was too late. Munger was already out the door. The young man kept a brisk pace, and Jack struggled to keep up. He could feel the muscles in his legs becoming weaker. His breath came in ragged gasps even though the walk was only about a mile out of town, just as the directions said. He was losing his youth, steadily, and fast. Only a few days earlier, Jack would have thought nothing of running twice the distance.

Far ahead, Munger turned down a dirt track. Jack followed. The wind hissed through the corn on either side of the road as the bank of clouds rolled closer. It looked like rain, maybe a lot of it.

Munger hurried down the path that sliced through the cornfield. Jack followed. Their destination was a small farmhouse that had not quite been finished. The roof was on, but the walls were not quite complete. A young couple stood in front, hands on their hips.

By the time Jack arrived, they had finished with pleasantries. "We need to be fast," Munger said gruffly to them. "Do you have the payment?"

The young husband handed over a small cloth bag. Munger's hands shook uncontrollably as he counted the coins. " "I'm doing this guy a favor, Jack thought to himself as he stopped just short of the transaction. This divining rod is going to eat him alive if I don't take it from him."

The dowser replied, "I'll be out of here in a minute. Dig where I say, and you'll have as much water as you need." Munger slung the leather bag from his shoulder, untied it, and removed the forked stick from its waterproof wrappings. He walked toward the barn and stopped at the split-rail fence. He draped the wrappings over the top rail and climbed through the fence. Then he held the twin prongs of the stick in his hands and walked into the field as if the forked stick pulled him along for the ride.

Jack shrugged an apology and tipped his hat to the young farm couple. He followed along behind the water witch. " "Might as well let this poor young couple get their money's worth, Jack thought."

The dowser walked slowly across the farmyard, his shoulders hunched and tense. He climbed through a wooden stockade and walked into the pasture. Jack stayed behind, leaning on the fence and watching.

The dowser walked a hundred yards out into the field and then slowed. He spun in place, pointing the stick this way and that.

Jack clambered through the fence and walked as fast as he could toward Munger. As he got closer, he thought he could hear the dowser moaning, as if in pain. Jack wasn't doing so well, either. His heart pounded painfully inside his chest. His legs shook with exhaustion.

Munger scrabbled at the ground, cutting a deep X into the dry dirt. When Jack reached his side, Munger gasped and fell to his knees, the dowsing stick on the ground in front of him. He pressed his palms against his temples and rocked back and forth slowly.

"Here it is!" he whispered hoarsely. "Tell them their well—all the water they want—is right here!"

"Having trouble with that branch, Mr. Munger?" Jack asked, moving warily closer.

The water witch struggled to his feet and rubbed his eyes. "I just need a second. No trouble—" He eyed Jack suspiciously. "You get old all of a sudden?" Another round of coughing tore through his body.

Jack stepped closer. "We both know why you've been so successful. But isn't it time you let those spirits rest? For your own sake, man. They're killing you just as sure as I'm standing here."

Munger took a few quick steps back toward the farmhouse, but Jack caught him by the arm and rasped urgently. "I've seen your house. You've made enough money to be very comfortable for the rest of your days. Give me the branch."

Mr. Munger tried to pull free, but he was too weak to break even Jack's feeble grasp. Munger shouted, "I need to put it away before—" Just then, lightning and thunder crashed above their heads as the wind whipped the farmer's field into a frenzy. "Let me go!" he shouted above the roar of the wind.

Jack used his free hand to snatch the branch from Munger.

In an instant, Jack was wide-eyed. Supernatural power ran through him like fire. He could hear the dowser, but he couldn't make out what he was saying over the shout of a young girl, a terrified scream in Jack's ears. Finally, her words, through the agony, became clear. "Water!" she shouted. "I'm burning! Please, someone! Help me!"

Images of a huge fire rushed through Jack's mind; a terrifying wall of flames collapsed around him like an avalanche, burning his skin and searing his hair. And the young girl, trapped inside that horrific memory, screamed for water, trapped inside this dry, forked stick. He knew then why Erastus Munger was such a successful dowser.

Through the disorienting pain, Jack was conscious of Munger shouting, "Give it back to me! The rain!"

Jack stumbled backward, but he held tight to the branch. They struggled for control of the haunted wood, their elbows and fists flying. In the midst of it all, the young girl's terrified screams seared through both of their minds like fire.

Lightning crashed above them.

"You don't understand," Munger shouted. "I need to wrap this stick up before—" Munger's fist caught Jack on the chin, knocking his head against the hard ground. But Jack hugged the stick close to his body as its power coursed through him. Jack could feel his clothes tighten, his arms and legs rippling once again with youthful strength.

In a minute, this Munger would be nothing that could hold him back, Jack knew. If only he could hold on that long. His body shook as the power threatened to rip him apart. His head spun inside the agony of the screaming voices, the single voice, among all the others, the girl screaming hoarsely for water.

Jack felt a weight lift from his chest, and then the little girl's voice was gone from his head. He shook himself alert and realized he was alone in the field.

He leaped to his feet, his young body nimble and alert. Munger ran unsteadily across the field toward the farmhouse carrying the forked branch in both arms as if it weighed a hundred pounds. He was halfway there.

Heavy drops of rain began to fall across Jack. It was too late to catch up to Munger, Jack knew. The line of rain pushed across the field, its large drops exploding like bombs in the dust, in pursuit, it seemed, of Munger. Then, with a loud clap of thunder, the clouds opened up.

A mad river of water fell from the sky. Jack ran across the muddy field after the dowser. A bright flash of lightning made him duck, and thunder crashed as if inside his own head.

He reached the spot where Munger had fallen. The water witch was slumped over the lower rail of the stockade fence, the forked stick on the ground in front of him, glistening with rainwater. The leather wrappings remained hung on the upper rail just out of reach when the rain arrived. Jack reached down to Munger and turned him roughly by the shoulders. The dowser's body slumped limply to the ground; a trickle of rain-splattered blood ran down his chin. His clenched fists had been burned black. His pouch split, spilling silver coins onto the mud.

Jack touched the stick, gingerly at first.

He felt nothing.

Then he picked it up.

As if from a great distance, he heard the laughter of a small girl who shouted, "Water! Mother, can you feel it? We're saved! Glorious rain!"

Jack held the branch high above his head as the rain cascaded down from the sky. Soon, the voices vanished completely, and Jack held in his hand a simple stick, worn smooth by months of handling, a plain branch from the north woods. Jack kicked at the bag that Munger carried the stick in. Too late for that now. The long agony of the young girl had been extinguished by pure, cold rain, just as Erastus Munger knew it would be if he hadn't been careful.

The farmhouse couple ran to them, alarm on their faces. Jack told them there had been an accident, told the wife to go get the sheriff. Then he led the husband out into the field and showed him the muddy X.

"Dig your well there," Jack said, looking at his youthful hands in wonder. "On good authority, I know there's plenty of water down there," he said.

The soaked farmer stood dumbfounded as Jack dropped the dowsing branch next to the lifeless body of Erastus Munger and just walked away, his hands wedged firmly into the pockets of his coat, as rain and lightning pelted the scene.

The sheriff would ask too many questions. Jack's stride was strong and youthful as his long legs propelled him from that little farm.

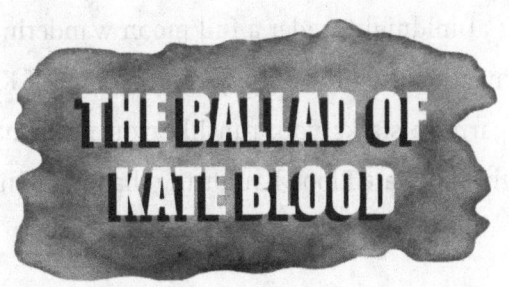

THE BALLAD OF KATE BLOOD

Riverside Cemetery in Appleton presents a compelling mystery for ghost hunters. This cemetery is a beautiful, old, and huge place filled with thousands of graves and tall trees. Away from the other stones, however, and much closer to the river than any other grave, rests the burial marker for a woman who was named Kate Blood. She is rumored to haunt the cemetery, especially at night, and especially on the night of a full moon. The story goes that Kate had a tough life, that her husband was abusive. Driven to irrational desperation one night, she took matters into her own hands and killed her husband and her children. Mad with guilt, she then killed herself. The people of Appleton buried her far from sanctified ground in a place that is even now obscured by a thick tangle of underbrush. The rumors of hauntings started soon thereafter. To this day, people out for a walk along the Fox River on a summer evening report strange sounds coming from this part of the woods: a woman laughing maniacally, footsteps across leaves and gravel, a low growl coming out of the darkness. Some report seeing a woman in a white dress beckoning to them, smiling seductively, her hands dripping blood. Needless to say, if you are out at midnight under a full moon wandering the trails along the river just east of Peabody Park, beware! If Kate Blood's ghostly apparition stalks you, run like you never have before. Run—the ghost of Kate Blood haunts the shadows of night!

THE WRONG SHADOW

Full moon tonight—I told Maggie we shouldn't sleep in this south-facing bedroom, but she didn't listen. She wants to be woken up by the sunrise, she says. The problem is now it's after one and I'm lying here awake, trouble rolling through my brain like the CN freight that rumbles right now through the Appleton night. A blast at every crossing from way up north as it diagonally southwest. A car with a bum wheel bangs its heel along the track for all to hear. Finally, with a single burst at the Outagamie crossing, the train is through for now. One more distant blast at the Prospect crossing, and that's it.

I had time this week to study the map, to find the active roads, to watch the trains out here as they pass. It's different here. Timber and paper. It's all intermodals and gondolas in Pennsylvania where I'm from.

These summers are going to kill me. How did she pick here? We could have lived anywhere after Becky died, but she picked Appleton out of the blue. We're from eastern Pennsylvania—both families live there, too—the Poconos. Green hills, waterfalls, great pizza—a fine place to raise a family. But now we won't. No chance of that.

Childless, sleepless, and alone, I slip out of bed and pad downstairs. I eat cereal and read yesterday's paper. A faint scratching I don't notice right away. All that train and mill noise, how could I pick that out? Mice in the walls? Summer brings out all kinds of life.

More scratching. It sounds like it is coming from the back door.

I freeze in my chair, the paper propped up against the cereal box. That doesn't sound like a mouse. I stand and edge toward the back door, waiting. A breeze rustles the trees, and the moon makes crazy shadows on the kitchen wall. That tapping again—I am sure now it's coming from outside. Maybe some crazy neighbor doesn't realize new people have moved into the house. I edge toward the door, careful not to make any noise or turn on the light.

Again, a tap at the door, this time more forcefully. A voice, too. A single word. I can't make it out. I put my ear to the door and listen. For a long time, nothing. Then, just as I am about to give up, the scratching comes again, as if someone were trying to scrape a thin crust off the outside of the door. And the voice again—a thin voice.

"Come."

My cereal is getting soggy. I have no time for mysteries.

Truth told, so what if it is a thief?

It would break the monotony.

A childless father, that's me.

What's that, you ask?

Good question.

A real good question.

I press my ear against the door once more.

Silence.

Five minutes.

Ten minutes.

Must be gone, so I turn on the outside light and open the door. Then I get mad at myself for being afraid. I fling it wide and step out into the night. Bugs have already begun to gather in the unexpected light, as if they were pilgrims at the right place and time for a visit by their god. Ah, bugs in the summer. If only there were something for people that matched what lights do to bugs.

Then I hear it—running feet down my driveway. I step to the side of the house quickly and follow. I round the corner and spot a small, shadowy figure at the end of the driveway who darts across the neighbor's lawn and down the street.

Moonlight fills the air—a muggy summer night. Crickets chirp, fans and air conditioners whir. But I made no mistake. It was a person. I walk down the driveway to the end and look south. In the distance, a figure walks quickly away from me. This is just getting too strange, I think. But I'm awake, I didn't start it, and as they say, everyone loves a good mystery.

Now, where have I heard that? Ah—Becky's favorite: Scooby-Doo. They say it for commercial breaks. Haven't seen that show in, well, I know exactly how long it has been.

Exactly.

Barefoot, I walk south down Outagamie Street, the moon lighting my path. I lose sight of the darting figure ahead of me at times, but when it emerges into the streetlight, there it is again. Dark and nimble. Walking, I won't catch up, I know that. Not unless the person stops. Then, I guess, we'll have a conversation.

I reach Alicia Park. Tall trees dapple the ground with moonlight. Shadows everywhere. I'll protect you, I told Becky. I'll always protect you.

Field trip to the waterfall. I wasn't there.

I was at work, of course.

She fell, and I didn't even find out until several hours later. Hours had passed when I was living my life while she was gone. I just didn't know.

In the copse of trees there in the middle of the park—is that the dark shape I have been chasing? And for what? Because they knocked? Is that all? "I'm here," I wanted to say. "I'm here if someone needs me."

Yes, it is the shadow I have been following. There, in the middle of the park, by those trees. The hard ground hurts my bare feet as I cut across the grass. I can't get close to these playsets without thinking. Monkey bars—she loved them. Tire swings? The best. And I loved them, too. No more.

I follow the shadow to the trees and stop. Nothing here. "Hey!" I whisper. Do I actually want to be answered? I don't know.

Nothing.

"Look, I know you're in there. I followed you here." I begin to move to the other side of the copse of trees. "I know you were at my door." The wall of green opens into a narrow gap, a door into a room made of foliage. "I'm not mad or anything." I push my head into the gap in the branches. "What did you want?"

The breeze hisses through the leaves above me, and it sounds like someone says, "Hush."

"Is someone there?" I ask in a normal speaking voice. No reply.

I have never been in this park, so close to my new home, and this little hill in the middle of these trees, so out of place. Strange little hill in a town so flat. I want to laugh, but I don't. I miss mountains, hills, anything other than the endless flat expanse of Appleton.

Then, as my eyes adjust to the filtered-moon darkness of the interior of the grove, the hill reveals its secret. A cave about three feet tall. How could that be? Crouched in front of it, the apparition I have been following. But the thing, whatever it is, shows no signs of seeing me. He or she or it or whatever just crouches at the cave entrance and peers inside.

I take one step toward the cave—a sharp pain radiates up through my foot. "Agh!" it must be glass. I try to see in the dimness the bottom of my foot. My attention, for a moment, is taken away from the cave. Yes, something cut my foot, but thankfully, I don't have the jagged shard of glass wedged into my tendons that I feared might be there. Just a small cut.

I remember again and look at the cave. The person is gone. Not gone, rather, inside. Or something is.

From within the dark recess of the cave are two eyes, orange, feral.

A bear? Dog? Not here, I reasoned. I can be very reasonable under pressure. That's one of the things my wife really resents about me. When she wants some company on the frantic side of town, I just get calm. Some people would appreciate that. Not Maggie.

So here I am with a throbbing foot, a yard away from the eyes of something dark and cave-dwelling.

I growl. If this thing wants to stare me down, I'd give it right back. Unless it is cornered. Then it will have no choice but to—

A hand on my shoulder. I spin on the dirt, crab away backward toward the cave, then, remembering the eyes, roll sideways. "Get away from me!" I scream, panting.

Framed by the moonlight behind him, the shadow stands just inside the grove of trees, his hands on his hips. "You're following the wrong shadow," he hisses.

Well, that is not what I expected. Out here in Appleton, of all places, far away from everything and everyone I have ever known, and to be told that? I say, "What are you trying to be, profound or something? Who told you to knock at my door?"

I'm close to the shadow now, but still, except for the voice, barely more than a ragged whisper, I can make out nothing. It is as if he is black, opaque, a void. The shadow dropped his hands to his sides. "See in there?" he points at the cave opening. I had forgotten for a moment about those eyes. Still there, though, malevolent, unblinking.

I swallow hard. "What is it?"

The shadow crouches down next to me. "Not what at all. Who."

"Answer me!" I growl, my voice shaking with anger and fear.

I can't look away from those eyes. They cut into me, as if they are shards of glass themselves. I squint in pain, but I don't close my eyes.

"Go ahead," the shadow whispers behind me. "Go ahead and crawl inside. It's not like you don't want to."

And when he says it, I know it's true. I do want to. Just crawl inside. Oblivion. Without willing it, I feel myself moving forward toward those eyes, pulled by an unseen energy inward.

I feel the shadow's hot breath on my shoulder. It whispers malevolently. "She needed you and you let her die." Closer. Behind my ear, only inches away. "You let her die. It's your fault."

One hand, then a knee, then the other hand and other knee, I'm crawling toward the cave opening. Yes, it is. It is my fault. My throat ties itself into a knot. My fault. I was too hard on her, made fun of her for being afraid, pushed her to take risks, saying that if you played it safe, nothing exciting would ever happen. They said she had climbed out onto the ledge to take a picture, to win the photography contest. To please me. They didn't say that, but I knew it. Maggie knew it, too.

Oblivion.

The end of all of this.

Maggie wouldn't miss me.

She'll be relieved.

"You killed her," the shadow whispered softly. "As if you pushed her yourself."

"Yes," I breathe. "Yes, it's true." My head is inside the cave now. I smell the damp earth, the remnants of fires, feel the heat from... where? Radiating across my skin, the eyes receding, calling to me, I reach forward into emptiness, the ground below me gives way.

I'm falling through darkness, searing heat, watched by eyes that have become great fires that scorch my skin. The screams of thousands shatter the night. My scream joins them—I think it does—too loud to tell for sure.

The shadow hurtles through the red space next to me, devoid of feature and temperature. "This is where you belong," it shouts.

And in anguish, my skin burning away from my body one layer at a time, hurtling downward, ever down, pursuing those eyes, pursued by that shadow, I fall and fall and fall and fall and fall and fall and fall and fall and fall and fall and fall and fall and fall.

Now, you'll think I am a fond, foolish, grieving father, but I swear to you what I am about to tell you is true: I hear my daughter's voice. She calls to me, "Daddy!" as clear as anything you've ever heard in your life.

There it is!

That voice.

Her voice.

Her small hand emerges from the red darkness above. I grasp it. The shadow cackles, "I have you!" but I hold onto that soft little hand for what little I'm worth.

I clench my eyes and hold on.

Time passes and the shouts quiet.

My sense of falling disappears.

Two ambulance guys prop me up against a tree, their hands on my shoulders, gentle voices bringing me out of sleep or whatever it was. It's daytime. How did that happen? And that cave? I spin around—the ambulance guys speak softly to me. The cave is right there. Small, shallow. Not at all like the night.

Maggie runs from the squad car. "Oh, Will! I was so worried!" and she kneels in the dirt next to me. Right there in the dirt.

I bury my head in her shoulder and from nowhere tears start to flow. I cry so much that the ambulance guys and the cops pack up their stuff and move away from us.

"My fault! It was my fault!" I sob into Maggie's shoulder.

She pushes me away from her with both hands. "Nobody's fault, you understand? It's nobody's fault. People live, people die. Becky died." She pulls me close again. "Nobody's fault," she whispers and rocks me gently.

When we get home, she helps me wash and puts me to bed even though it is morning.

I tell her all I can of the night before, but I forget part of it until she draws the shades and is at the door ready to pull it shut and let me sleep.

"The shadow," I say. "It was here last night. At our door."

"I know. Dreams are like that sometimes."

"But it wasn't—"

"Shh," she coos and holds my hand in hers. She pushes a wisp of hair from my eyes and smiles sweetly.

All at once I remember that I have not yet slept. Fatigue covers me like a cool blanket. The fear of falling, the terrifying voices, for the moment, they fade. Happy to be safe at home with Maggie, I open my eyes to thank her.

I don't get the words out. Instead, my throat tightens in terror.

Maggie's face glows strangely in the muted light, her eyes distant, unblinking, otherworldly.

I swear what I am about to tell you is true, even though you may think me insane.

No one else is there, so you need to believe me.

She says, without even the faintest emotion, the smallest portion of tenderness, she says exactly what that malevolent voice said at the open maw of the pit. "You're following the wrong shadow," she says coldly. And then she pulls the door shut, leaving me alone in the room.

With the blunt solidity of fear crushing my chest, I pull the blanket up to my chin and listen as she walks down the hall and down the stairs, until the sound she makes is nothing more than a faint thud, a gentle tapping, as if someone were trying to scrape away the thin crust that protects something fragile, something rare, something irreplaceable.

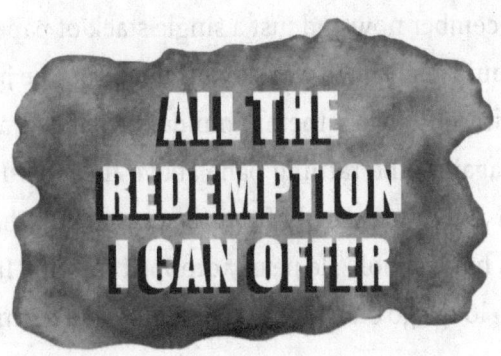

ALL THE REDEMPTION I CAN OFFER

Professor David Hastings was a very old man—he'd tell you so himself. At times, his mind wandered. At times, he forgot even where he was, but at least that might be excused. For many decades, he had been a professor at another, more prestigious university in the East. Out with the old, his young English Department colleagues said, and they wined and cheesed him out the door one bright morning last May.

But David didn't feel finished. Not yet, anyway. Not with his life's work still ahead of him. He decided to start again somewhere else, a place where he could find what he was looking for. He pared everything he owned down into a single suitcase and several boxes of books and papers, and took the best part-time job he could find on short notice. He spent a day in late August moving into the old house in Appleton, five blocks from campus. He didn't know a soul.

The students at Lawrence were nice enough and filled with those Midwestern good manners that bordered on disinterest. And his colleagues—those that knew him at all—were nice enough too. They had even given him Gothic Lit, a course David could do in his sleep (and at times feared he might have).

Mid-December now and just a single stack of papers to grade before he could get back to work on his novel, but he just couldn't convince himself to start them. Thunder crashed as a cold wind drove rain against the rattling pane above the sink. He stood in the kitchen and drank deeply from the crystal cup that he'd had forever. His hand shook. He nearly dropped the cup. Its twin had shattered so long ago on a night David didn't like to think about.

Fifty years earlier, Libby went away. He didn't understand why at the time, but the answer was coming. He could feel it. Something he said had made her angry. His defense of the remark enraged her further. She left his house, tearful, frantic, after the crystal glass shattered against the wall behind him. David's ego prevented him from following her.

Of such small stuff lives are made and unmade.

Morning came, and he swept the shards of glass into the can.

He called her, visited her room in the grad students' dorm.

Her things were gone.

He asked everywhere.

He never saw her again.

He supposed he should have tried to find her, gone to the bus station, asked around, but he convinced himself he was the aggrieved one, and for months afterward, he sank himself into his dissertation: Carl Jung, Gothic depictions of the fertility deity archetype, and the huge head that drops into the castle on the eve of Theo's wedding in Walpole's The Castle of Otranto. David let the memory of Libby slip beneath committee assignments, readings, lectures, and tenure. He became a leading figure in his field.

All those years, though, in summers and Christmases ever since, he had worked on this other story, the novel that remained forever elusive to him. There it lay in his kitchen, now in Appleton, of all places, like any other dead thing, David thought. Six big boxes of sketches, drafts, notes, and photocopied pages from various newspapers over the years. All leading exactly nowhere. But he still had hopes.

Wind rattled the old windows and thunder rumbled in the distance. While the tea kettle heated, David opened the first paper. It discussed the disembodied voice of Rochester in Jane Eyre and how it motivated Jane's action. Halfway through, the paper shifted abruptly to a discussion of the ghosts in Hamlet. David laughed quietly. The dynamic avengers of literature, Jane and Hamlet, pushed by supernatural forces to wreak havoc on their worlds. One (Jane), hems and haws, the other (Hamlet) becomes a killing machine ("constant practice"). David let the paper fall back on the table without grading it. He walked to the stove to check on his tea water. Only thirty more papers to go just like that.

Strange, he thought. The heat under the tea kettle was still off, and his water was cold. He was sure he had turned it on. "Ah, me," David sighed, "I am a fond, foolish old man." He turned the stove heat back on and picked the next paper out of the pile. "Consciousness and Ghostliness: A Haunting of the Self by the Self" started off moderately interesting, with the assertion that the actor who plays the character of Hamlet can find cues in the text to show that he is supposed to be aware that he is inhabiting another character, and that all the other "people" in the play are just characters, too. That was the first paragraph. At least this paper showed a glimmer of understanding. That is, until the second paragraph. The paper then veered off into a study of the nature of consciousness using Sartre and Malcolm X as case studies to illustrate "multifarious relegations" or somesuch. He held the pencil poised over the final page.

He was tired of grading.

Tired of it all.

His eyes unfocused.

He might have drifted off to sleep.

A burning smell? David turned in his chair—the blue flame glowed brightly under the tea kettle, and something like steam poured forth from the spout—but it didn't whistle. David lurched over to the stove and recoiled sharply when his hand touched the handle. It was glowing hot. He switched off the stove and, using a towel, knocked the kettle into the sink. He sprayed cold water on it and watched as the steam obscured the window glass. He rubbed his eyes. If only these students would write something new and different somehow, to take the ideas he has been rehashing these many years and run with them. If only.

He gave up on tea and had a long drink of cold water instead. He fingered the crystal glass and tried to focus on the papers. He actually got through some of them. The clock chimed for midnight. The rain intensified. Lightning flashed into his room, and thunder rumbled as if someone were rolling a heavy barrel across his roof.

At first, he didn't hear it. The sound of it mixed with the near-constant thunder.

But there it was again: a knock at the front door.

Curious, David tilted his head, raised his nose. No one had ever knocked before.

He opened the front door to find a pretty young woman under the cover of the porch pulling off her hood and unzipping her coat.

"That rain!" she whispered. "Can I come in, Professor? It's very cold out here."

David thought her face looked familiar—maybe a student of his? "Of course, my dear," he said.

She brushed past him and hung her coat on a peg in the hall, then turned to him. "I saw your light on—I hope I didn't wake you." She ran her fingers through her long blonde hair and smiled. A gold cross hung on a chain from her neck.

David cleared his throat. "What brings you out on a night like this?"

She tilted her head coquettishly. "I always walk at night. This rain, though. I am cold all the way through. Do you have anything hot to drink? Or a blanket?" She used her elbow to push open the door to his bedroom. "Whoops!" she said, laughing. He was glad he had spent part of that morning cleaning. At least his bed was made.

"I'm just grading papers," he said. "But I'll put on some tea."

She walked down the hall to the kitchen, slow and dreamy. David rubbed his chin. Something about her.

She stood above the stack of papers and poked through them. "Any good ones?"

"Is yours in there?" he asked. That question, no matter what answer it got, he could use.

"Mine? No."

"What's your name?" he pounced.

She smiled sweetly at him. "Do names really matter? We're here—"

"Your name, please," he said tensely. He was accustomed to being in charge, to wielding the power that comes from spending a life at the front of a classroom. Age diminishes that, too, he had found.

She frowned and held up one index finger. "First, I want to thank you for getting me out of the storm. I had nowhere else to go, and you opened your home to me." Her blue eyes glittered, flecks of rainwater shone like diamonds in her hair. She tilted her head upward.

Something inside of him—something that felt old, dusty, and gray—began to crank to life. His feet tingled.

"But what should I call you?" he whispered.

"Matilda," she breathed, and raised her mouth toward his.

He stepped backward in surprise. "I knew it!" he shouted triumphantly. "I knew it!"

He went to the hallway and came back with her things. "The Monk, the great Matthew Gregory Lewis, who wrote his life's work in ten weeks at the age of nineteen. You, Matilda, the seductress sent by Satan himself to undo the good monk, Ambrosio. It went all bad for Ambrosio once he let that" (he punctuated the next three words while handing the woman her coat, hat, and gloves) "charming... little... girl... under his skin." He held the kitchen door open for her. "Please leave my house and do not return. I am a busy man."

She frowned and took up her coat and hat. She walked to the front door, placed her hand on the knob, and turned to face him. Her eyes flashed with danger. "The chance to enter into one of the books you love so much—how can," she ran her finger along the outline of his ear, "how can you pass up that chance, mi Ambrosio?"

"But you aren't even real," he whispered, marveling that only now had he considered the strangeness of a character coming to life. "How could you be?" He looked into her youthful eyes and studied the smooth skin of her face. He felt the heat of her body radiate through him. He raised his hand to touch her cheek, swallowed the lump in his throat. Matilda destroyed Ambrosio in the novel, yes, but the intensity of it all. The chance to flame out in a screaming meteor of glory across life's sky. What would that be worth?

He let his hand drop.

"No, my dear Matilda. No more. I am not the man I once was." He let the screen door close gently between them.

She walked out onto the porch and down the steps. The cold rain darkened her shoulders and hat. At the bottom of the steps, she turned to face him. "You may yet meet me, Ambrosio."

"It will be the first time, my sweet little hallucination," he said and closed the door gently behind her. He pressed his forehead against the cold wood of the door and clenched his teeth. This past month, he had been having more trouble than usual keeping in focus what was real and true.

He must be dreaming now.

That's it.

A dream.

He stood up straight and smoothed his vest. He slapped his cheeks gently. I feel awake, he thought. He flexed his stiff fingers and bit his pinky. No waking up from this one. He returned to the kitchen, resolved to finish the terrifying pile of student papers.

"Ah! There's the rub! What if I dream, I have graded these papers and then wake to find I have not even begun? Can I recover from that?" he laughed.

Footfalls in the kitchen. David opened the door and gasped in surprise. A man, with his back to him, was in the corner by the window reading something. Not just something—David's novel!

The top box of the stack was open, and the man held wrinkled and yellow pages in each hand.

"Please put my work back where it belongs," David calmly said.

The man turned to face him. He was wearing a brown tweed jacket with tan elbow patches. His reading glasses hung at the tip of his long nose. Oiled gray hair shone in the kitchen lamplight. "Belongs? In this box?" He sniffed. "I shan't say I disagree."

David stood rigidly. That particular box held pages from the initial burst of creativity that came after Libby's departure. No one had looked in there in many, many years, not even David himself. Something about it was unapproachable. It was at the same time the source of all his hope and the storehouse of despair. He feared for what he would find if he opened that box again. "Please return those pages to where you found them."

The man huffed and continued reading. "It says here—and how can this be serious? —that she—and I quote—'radiated the very ecstasy of life's possibility.'" He tilted his head and regarded David above his reading glasses. "Is this satire?"

Anger flashed inside David. "What gives you the right to read my private papers?"

The man laughed, "Oh, my dear professor, your literary executor will do it, of course." Then he frowned and looked David up and down. "And I daresay soon."

David walked to the man's side and took the pages, careful not to look at them. He gently shouldered the man away from his stack of boxes. "Let him wait."

"But you haven't even worked on this in years! When do you plan to let your adoring public see your crowning achievement?"

David knew the man was baiting him, wanted to see him lose his temper. Instead, David smiled calmly. "When it is ready and no sooner."

The man walked to the kitchen sink. "But your legacy," the man said as he inspected the crystal cup. "What of that?" the man held the crystal glass up to the light.

David replaced the lid on the box and spun to face the man, his eyes burning. "Yes, you keep saying that. Three books from Oxford University Press, you probably know, is no small thing. One a seminal work in the Gothic, or so says Harold Bloom."

"Bloom! That mildewed corpse? He'd blurb a tsunami."

"Nevertheless, I stand by my professional legacy!" David spat, and suddenly the room spun. He sat heavily in his chair and rubbed his eyes. The night air pressed in all around him and made it hard to breathe. "And you don't even exist. Why am I defending my life against a shade?"

Into David's ear the man whispered, "Nothing. A blank. That is your professional legacy."

An instant tranquility replaced the uneasiness David had felt earlier. "Is that all? Disparage my work? Sure, go ahead. It is an easy target, I suppose. But I tried my best, and I can go to my grave knowing I tried my best."

"Grave? Well, who said anything about that? You're jumping the start, David." The man sat down at the table across from David. "And trying is not the measure of a man given the gifts you have been given. Yours was to succeed, to finish your true life's work."

David looked wearily at the stack of boxes in the corner. "I know I have failed, mostly," he said meekly.

"Blast it all!" the man thundered, leaping from his seat. "Rage, rage against the dying of the light!" He stormed to the hallway and pulled open the front door. "I give up on you, my dear professor. To have so little regard for what you have been given... I didn't think it possible!" He opened the front door wide. The gale blew rain into the front hall.

David lurched to the door, pressed it almost closed, and watched through the crack as the strange man stopped on the grass and raised his arms. Lightning flashed through him as if he were somehow not all there. He raised his eyes to the sky and shouted, "He is as you said, broken beyond mending."

Lightning crashed right on top of the house, it seemed, and thunder shook the knob out of David's hand. And when he blinked away raindrops, the man on the lawn was gone.

Shaken, David closed the door and returned to the kitchen. He stood at the table, fists on either side of the piled papers, and clenched his eyes shut. The man certainly seemed real. But he knew it was an impossibility. He graded more papers. He must have closed his eyes. The clock chimed two. He awoke to the pile of student papers, with half remaining to be graded.

"Why aren't these ever imaginary?" he chuckled.

He sat heavily in his chair and began one that compared yellow wallpaper to the white whale and Young Goodman Brown's desire to a journey into the forest, dark and deep. The life, the creativity of the idea made him smile. This was a student who knew a little bit about how to approach life, how to make something from nothing. David wrote, "The trick in life is not to avoid white whales and wallpaper, but to surrender yourself to them. We all die, but only the unhappy few die with the profound regret of not doing what it is we were born to do. Grade: A."

Five uninspired papers later, he closed his eyes. Only two more to go, then he could rest.

He lifted his head and there, at the table across from him, sat, well, himself.

David (himself) coughed hard and couldn't catch his breath.

David (his other self) waited patiently; his hands folded on the table in front of him.

"We're dying," his other self said. "And I tried hard to help, I really did."

David leaned closer. The man across from him was certainly him, but younger. That was the only difference. The deep creases on his own cheeks and chin were not yet there. The eyes were more alive, clear, and piercing.

"For most people, it is not so hard to cling to life. You, well, you don't seem to care either way."

This was all too much. David's outward calm fractured, and he shouted, "And why should I? That young woman just now, what is she but a reminder that I am old?" He rubbed his chest and tried to calm himself down. His voice shook with emotion. "And that man! He did nothing but remind me what I already know, that I have failed my talent, that I am alone and deserve as much." He sprang from his seat and lurched to the sink unsteadily. "I already know all of that. The sacrifices I have made? And to get where? Shown the door on a May afternoon," he said. He filled the crystal cup again with water. He drank one cup and then another, but he couldn't slake his thirst. "My portrait hangs in the library, my books decay, ignored in the stacks? But I'm still here. And for what? To carry ten thousand pages of regret, to carry all that like my albatross. One night where I chose wrong and I can never, never get it back."

Lightning flashed weakly; its blue light shattered inside the crystal in his hand. A flash of insight, too: That light, he thought, like the choices we make, ramify in all directions, never to return to the source inside that cloud, absorbed by the earth, dissipating in the roll of thunder across this forsaken prairie, split into uncountable paths all by the accident of my hand holding up this cup at this moment.

He turned to his younger self and smiled. "How unlikely. Light, the primal force of nature, yet subject to my thoughtless action." Clutching the back of his chair, he thrust his face at his younger self. "I altered the course of lightning with this cup. I did. And yet something as delicate as a thoughtless decision I am powerless to bend."

His younger self exhaled loudly. "Are you arguing that mere accident could bring a man given a fine mind and a real chance at love to this lonely and bitter end? Mere accident? No conscious choice? After all this time? You share no responsibility at all?"

David fell to his seat exhausted. "Yes, oh, sure. But it's semantics at that point, isn't it? With incomplete information, how can a man be fully responsible for his choices?"

His younger self shook his head in sorrow. "There are some things we can never recover from. But if you could do all again, where would you begin? What would you leave done?"

David tried to swallow the lump in his throat, but it stayed stuck. He closed his eyes and tried to breathe, but it came with difficulty. The clock chimed three. Everything hurt. Finally, he breathed again without difficulty, as if the storm had passed.

A soft voice, "David."

He lifted his head.

There, looking at him with rage in her eyes, she was.

"Libby."

She hadn't aged much in all these years. She sat with arms crossed and wild eyes. "You son of a bitch," she hissed. "All this time, and this is what you've made of yourself?"

David stared at her, his mouth agape. Those other three, they were bad enough. But now his wandering mind made ridiculous sport with him. "Look," he said, grasping tightly the edges of the table. "I don't mean to be rude, but I really need to finish grading these papers, so if you'll excuse me..."

Libby leaped to her feet. "No!" she shouted. "You will answer for what you did! I have been waiting years—decades, you broken, old man, for this moment. You will not ruin it for me."

David regarded her quizzically. "Waited for this?" he asked gently.

Libby walked to the stacked boxes and stood with her back to him. "You abused me."

David thought hard. "No, I did not. It was you who abused me. When you left—"

Libby spun savagely. "When I left? It was you who forced me out. Forced me out on the night I had to—"

David said softly, "Go ahead. Say what you planned to say."

"I had to tell you something."

David didn't have to try hard to remember the details of the night. It had been a difficult week for both of them. Libby had been especially on edge, blaming David for things he could not possibly have done, lashing out at him for little or no reason. In retrospect, he knew he wasn't the easiest person in the world to get along with, but Libby had been positively vitriolic that week.

When she left, it was almost a relief. But then he had missed her dearly. "Tell me now."

Libby walked to him, loomed over him, her shoulders tense, her fists balled at her hips. Her youth and rage could overwhelm David, he knew. He braced for the assault. Please, make it quick. If there is more, I need to atone for, he thought, let it be quick.

Libby leaned close. "I had to tell you... Not that you had room in your life as a literary superstar for anything that mundane. I knew you would have seen it as my failing somehow, that you would have condemned me for it like you did for everything else."

David sat back in his chair, the truth rising slowly like the dawn in the east. "What happened?" he asked, his mind racing.

Libby's exhaled sharply. "What happened? Your son is what happened, you selfish old man. Your son."

David pressed his palms against his eyes. This couldn't be real. Another trick of his mind. It had to be. But when he opened his eyes again, there she was.

Libby.

Furious.

She leaned forward and yelled, "He grew to be the most wonderful man on the face of the earth. He got awards, saved lives, made people happy."

David gasped. "Where is he?"

"You want to meet him?" Libby smiled sweetly, but her eyes shone like fire. "You want to meet him?" she spat.

David leaned closer, tried to take her hand. "My son... Of course I want to meet him. Why didn't you tell me sooner?"

Libby shook all over, her chin quivering. Tears welled up in her eyes.

"Why didn't you tell me about our son?"

Libby put both hands into her eyes and screamed. "I can't do it! Don't make me do it!" She ran into the hallway and pressed her forehead against the front door glass. "Please! Don't make me do it!"

David followed her and put his hand on her shoulder. "It's okay. Just, please..." David had never been good at consoling, but Libby seemed so shattered he couldn't help but feel broken right along with her. He felt the bony curve of her shoulders under her clothes, just the way he remembered her. "You don't need to do anything tonight. Just rest."

Libby whispered, "I couldn't tell you. I was so scared. I wanted to tell you, but you were so driven, so focused. I didn't want to be blamed for—I don't know." She pushed him away, looked into his eyes. "I drove for two days. I didn't even know where I was. The desert. That's all I knew. I tried to kill our baby. I bled to death in a motel room. I watched as my body bled to death. I was so full of anger—I hated you from that moment. I waited and waited, then I found you here tonight. I wanted to kill you, to make you suffer for what you did. I wanted to tell you about our son, make him real for you, and then kill him in front of your eyes. Make you suffer the way I did. But now you're just a nice, old fool, and I can't do it. Everything I planned, the young girl, the reviewer, even facing you at your worst—all of it."

David pulled her close to him. "Shh, my gentle little Libby. I have lived many, many years and have learned a few things about what is important."

Libby sobbed, "I wanted you to die miserably."

"You'll never know how much I have missed you all these years. You were the only one, Libby. My only one. Can you ever forgive me?"

Libby stopped crying. She wiped her eyes on his sweater. "I'm so mixed up. I've been angry with you for so long. I almost apologized to you just then."

He laughed quietly.

"Why are you laughing?" she whispered.

"Because this reminds me of so many days and nights when we fought and then made up. Ah, Libby, I am so sorry for everything. I know I wasn't easy to live with. I had other priorities, I know. But if I could do it all again, I would tell you I love you every moment of every day. You're the only one. The only one."

Libby relaxed in his arms. "I do remember being there in the hotel hating you, dreaming of revenge. Now I am here. I don't know where the years went."

"Ah, my sweet, sweet Libby," David cooed. "Redemption arrives like a stranger at your door in a storm. How many of us are wise enough to let her in?"

Libby raised her eyes. "I do feel redeemed somehow. More peaceful. Oh, David, something is calling me. Someone. Let me up! I have to go!"

David heard the voice, too. A loving voice, caring and soft. From just on the other side of the door. Libby helped him to his feet. "We need to go now!"

David felt his chest tighten. His breathing came ragged and hard. He looked into Libby's eyes and felt the warm rush of love flow back through his bones. "Please," he said. "I need five more minutes."

Libby took his hand in hers. "I'll wait for you," she said. "But only five minutes!" The clock chimed six.

David shuffled back into the kitchen and read the final student paper, a study of Shirley Jackson's approach to architecture. The kid was an engineering student, David knew. A good blend of interests, and he told him so in his comments, all positive. He recorded the last of the grades in his book and stood from the table. His old legs were stiff and sore. The night storm had given way to a bright, Appleton December morning that filtered through frosted windowpanes.

He filled the crystal cup one last time and drank deeply. He felt the cold water flow through him, down into his legs and arms, until his body tingled with life.

He looked down at his hands. His hair in this strange light looked dark and full, as if he had the arms of a young man.

He placed the crystal cup on the sill where it caught the sunlight and sprayed rainbows across the room.

His legs felt strong.

He looked one last time back into the kitchen. It was a good house, a good final stop. Good kids, his students. All of them over the years.

There in the middle of the kitchen, the stack of graded papers neatly piled, the pen capped, he was not surprised to see the body of an old man slumped in his chair.

David smiled and nodded. "That's it, then." The boxes of notes and papers—what he mistakenly thought was his life's work— loomed dully against the kitchen's white wall.

He shut off the light and closed the door.

Libby waited for him at the front door. "Do you hear that?" she asked excitedly.

David listened intently. Again, the soft voice returned, calling, David! Elizabeth!

"I do," he replied. "What do you want to do?"

Libby smiled happily. "Oh, for once I get to decide?"

"You're the redemption that came knocking at my door tonight."

She grasped the knob. "Okay, old man. But just know this. Coming here tonight, I feel like I'm the one who needed redemption. And I came to the right place."

The voice, a young man's voice, called to them. They opened the door into the sky-blue Appleton morning. A cold north wind blasted them. All around, the rain had frozen into diamonds that hung from the branches, into ice that coated everything, so that in the sunshine it was as if the two of them were very small and they had fallen into sun-soaked crystal glass.

THE TELULAH PARK LOCOMOTIVE

One evening last summer, I met an old man in Telulah Park on the walking path near the giant black locomotive. He stopped as I approached, leaned on his battered walking stick, waited for me, his mouth open, ready to speak. "After the Great Peshtigo fire," he began, grasping me by the sleeve, "this train right here brought timber to Vulcan—don't let the date on the sign fool you—it was hell itself that opened up that day—" the man was out of breath, impossibly old, he looked.

I looked for a polite way to extricate myself from the conversation to continue my bike ride. But the ancient man continued: "The people ran, but there was nowhere to go," he continued. "A couple of trains got out, that's all. The people stuck back there, amid that hellish inferno, they discovered the one way out that remained for them. They lived in that great white pine forest. That old wood had powers."

All right, I thought. Now he has me. I'm a sucker for a good story, and I was going nowhere in particular.

"That white pine forest, the oldest life on Earth still surviving, invited those poor people in. Not for all time, just for some time.

To protect them. To help them. That's how trees are," the old man's fingers dug into my forearm. "But trees move at a different speed than the rest of us. While only a moment passed for them, years passed for the rest of us.

"Before the trees got the chance to release the people, loggers arrived like locusts and tore the forest out by its roots. The wood—that haunted wood—cut and lumbered, milled and pulped, spread out across this wide land the spirits of terrified men, women, and children of Peshtigo, the fire still burning in their minds because that's how the trees felt it. And what was made from that wood held those spirits trapped, unholy prisons made of paper and grain. And this locomotive," the old man spun me—he was stronger than he looked—" this locomotive, driven by the devil himself, dragged those tenders full of human souls to mills across the Fox River Valley and helped spread all of that terror... Imagine watching your family burn, feeling the flames licking at your back, the air sucked from your lungs. All of that, this locomotive brought here, and more. But I trapped it here. I did it. I built this enclosure, tore up the rails. I did all of that." And it was true—the sidetrack was gone just as it broke free of the main line, at the south edge of Telulah Park. Grass grew where it once ran. "I did that for revenge!" he hissed.

The old man's hand fell from my arm. Strange that there would be a huge locomotive here in a city park. I had wondered about that. I marveled at the size of the boiler—huge and black. I imagined it hurtling through the night belching flames and sparks as it roared across the fields and forests of Northeast Wisconsin.

"Okay, boss," I said. "That's a good story, but—" and he was gone. I'm not saying that he walked away, I am saying that he was just gone, just like that. On the grass next to the path was his walking stick. I reached down to pick it up, but as my fingers touched it, I recoiled in pain. The wood itself was roaring hot! Not only that, but I got the weirdest sensation, as if I had seen something that wasn't there, a wall of fire and smoke, just like the old man said. I looked around; there was no one in the park but me. I crouched next to the walking stick and poked it with my finger. It was now only warm. I picked it up gingerly and felt again the strange tingle through my fingers, felt something distant and far away recede into nothingness. Then the feeling went away.

The stick was just a stick, no longer warmer than it should be.

I took it and held it in my hands.

A fine grain—pine, unless I was mistaken.

I tossed the piece of wood inside the train's enclosure. Just for a moment, it seemed as if the locomotive whispered to me, as if its boiler was coming back to life.

No. Impossible, I thought, but there it was again: a voice like the distant night wind. "Free me..." it hissed.

I pedaled away on my bike, the voice fading, although not vanishing, behind me...

THE KAUKAUNA GHOSTS

"Hold my hand—it's just a little bit farther," he said. The forest around the two young people hissed in the afternoon west wind that carried with it the electric scent of an approaching summer storm.

Dorothy reached up for Dwight's hand and let herself be pulled up the embankment. "If it's too far, I'll have to stop and rest," she said coyly. Strange boy, she thought. They were already well out of sight of the nearest house. No need to keep going like this. He's acting as if his story is true and not just a pretense to get her out there in the woods. "I don't think I can go any—" but she didn't finish the sentence. Instead, she stood, mouth open in surprise, at Dwight's side.

"I told you." Dwight beamed at her. "I told you it would be neat, didn't I?"

Dorothy took a few tentative steps toward the old house in the woods that loomed ahead of them. Dilapidated gables thrust their gray angles to the sky. The porch wrapped around the entire old house, but it sagged in places, as if the house were shrugging it off somehow, an unnecessary second skin. "I've never seen anything like it." She shook her head in wonder. "Does anyone live there?"

Smiling, Dwight took her hand and pulled her along toward the ramshackle wreck.

"But why is it off here in the woods like this so far from town?" she asked as they stopped at the foot of the porch steps.

Dwight shook his head. "My guess is that this was cleared land at some point. I bet this was a farmhouse that somehow just got left behind." Dwight placed one foot on the bottom step. Dorothy gasped in surprise, but the step held his entire weight. "Come on, try it," he said. "I'll go all the way up if you will."

Dorothy looked over her shoulder from where they'd come. They were on a high point on the bluff above the Fox River, just downstream from the mills and shops of Kaukauna. But up there in that patch of woods, it was as if the rest of the world had fallen away, and all that remained was that house and Dwight. A thrill went through her body, a tingling that brought goose bumps to her arms. "I don't know," she said. "I mean, can I trust you?"

"What's there to trust?" Dwight asked mischievously. The second step groaned beneath his weight, but the old wood held. He looked ahead at the closed door and swallowed nervously until he remembered that he had to act confident in front of the new girl at school. "Let's go inside. Come on in," he made a scary face, started talking like Bela Lugosi at the drive-in. "I dare you!"

High school was a tough place to make new friends, especially in a small town. At this stage in their lives, a new kid was pretty much the only topic of conversation in the lunchroom. They had already talked about most everything else. And from the first moment he saw her enter his history class a few weeks back, with her shy smile and bright blue eyes, Dwight had been smitten. He dreamed of the day he would talk to Dorothy; the day he might spend some time with her. Holding hands was positively out of the question, but now, when he looked down at the end of his arm, there was Dorothy's hand right there in his. Could it get any better? And a mysterious house to occupy their attention? Dwight figured he was just about the luckiest guy in the whole world at that moment.

Dorothy scanned the western sky. "Looks like it might rain," she said.

"All the better!" Dwight smiled. He scampered up the rest of the steps and turned to face her from the rotting porch. "Time to get in out of the storm." He held out his hand to her.

If Dorothy didn't know better, she might be a little bit afraid. But Dwight was a perfect gentleman at school, and the walk today revealed to her that he was sensitive and smart. This adventurous streak, well, who wouldn't love that?

Thunder rumbled in the distance, and the colorful leaves turned bottoms up in the wind. "Okay," she said tentatively. "The stairs look sturdy enough." She reached out for Dwight's hand and tiptoed up the stairs. When she got to the top, Dwight pulled her close. She smelled the cream in his hair, his aftershave, felt the rough collar of his cotton shirt, his strong, bony shoulder. A cold wind shivered her closer to him, and him to her.

Dwight put his hand around Dorothy's waist. "See? Nothing to be afraid of," he said. He turned her toward the front of the house, and they pressed their faces against the glass. They peered through the dirty windowpane but could see nothing in the darkness behind the grime.

Shadows fell around them as the sun was obscured by a thick blanket of dark clouds.

But Dorothy and Dwight hadn't noticed. They remained glued to that spot. Their hips were touching, and neither wanted to break the electric bond that had sprung between them.

Suddenly, from above them, came a scraping roar, as if something old and huge were grinding its teeth. Dorothy spun around in alarm. Dwight turned, too, but his heel caught on a nail, and he stumbled against the side of the house. He fell in a heap at the front door. "Ow!" he groaned.

Dorothy crouched at his side, trying not to laugh. "Are you okay?"

Dwight sat up and rubbed the top of his head, their voices lost in the hiss and scrape that seemed to come from every direction. "I just didn't know what—that noise!" And he looked out from the house into the woods. Dorothy turned to look, too. The ground had become gray, moving toward white, as if a dirty snow was falling right there in the middle of September.

"Hail!" Dorothy said, her word punctuated by a flash of lightning.

Dwight whistled in admiration. "Those stones are huge."

And at that moment, the gutter that ran along the front of the house, burdened by the weight of the sudden downpour of ice, tore loose from the roof and clattered down to the steps in front of them. They both leaped to their feet and into each other's arms. Nearby thunder crashed all around, as if to crush the ancient house with sound alone. The roof groaned as if it, too, would fall under the weight of the storm.

Dwight squeezed Dorothy's hand. "We have to get out of here!" he shouted above the roar of the storm, the eerie moan of the house.

Dorothy pulled him close. "We can't go out there. The storm's right on top of us!"

Dwight nodded seriously. "Okay. But we can't stay on this porch, either. It's liable to collapse."

He led her to the front door and tried the knob. He wasn't sure whether he was happy or afraid when it turned easily in his hand. In a sudden strong gust, the door ripped from his hands and swung inward with a crash. Dwight and Dorothy followed, as if pushed by that same wind. They staggered into the darkness of the house; the afternoon light, already dimmed by the storm, was no match for the dirty windows. They stopped, scarcely breathing, and waited for their eyes to adjust.

In the failing light, they could make out the large front room of the farmhouse, empty, except for a single chair that faced the hearth, its high back toward them. A narrow staircase ascended into darkness to their left, and the center hallway of the house ended in a door. Lightning flashes illuminated the outline of that door. Dwight clenched his teeth at the sight of it.

"You know, in a ghost story, something would be sitting in that chair," Dorothy shouted above the roar of the storm.

Dwight pushed the door closed and smiled in the dimness. "You saw *Psycho*!" he exclaimed. He saw in her eyes that she was proud that he had noticed. It was the scariest movie of the fall of '60, after all. Wind pushed the door ajar again. "Hmm. The latch must not be working," Dwight said. The door creaked on ancient hinges, moved by the unseen hand of the wind.

"I didn't even blink. I loved every second of it." Dorothy grinned proudly. "Are you going to check that chair or am I?"

Dwight felt himself falling for this girl he hardly knew. *Psycho* without blinking? Too good to be true! He took her hand—any excuse would do. "I dare you."

She didn't know where her courage came from. In truth, the movie had given her nightmares for weeks. A spooky chair in a haunted house in a thunderstorm with a stranger? What was she doing? But a calm came over her. She felt strange, as if she were invulnerable somehow. She shook off his hand and strode to the chair.

He didn't move. He wanted to move, wanted to be brave, wanted to show Dorothy that he wasn't afraid, but he felt as if his feet were nailed to the floor.

She passed the chair, turned to face it. She raised her hands to her mouth, her eyes wide in alarm, and drew in her breath sharply.

He stood transfixed. He wanted to run away or run to her or something but could not. Dorothy screamed in terror, staggered away from the chair.

He took one step backward toward the door, then, only because he willed it with all his courage, ran to her. He took her roughly by the shoulders and pushed her behind him, faced whatever terror was in that chair.

Through his blinking eyes, he looked down at the tattered fabric on the ancient chair. The pattern was vaguely floral, the coloring dusty pale yellow. Intersecting and coiling lines on the fabric gave the pattern depth somehow, as if he were looking into the chair and not just at it. But the plain fact was that the chair was empty. No one's decomposed mother rested there, coiled, ready to spring. No monster from hell, no vampires, no zombies, or anything else that crawled out of a Saturday morning double feature.

Behind him, Dorothy laughed. "I got you!" she whispered in his ear. "You were really afraid, weren't you?"

He turned, ready to be mad, but his anger melted when he gazed at her face. "I wasn't afraid. I mean, I knew you were afraid, so I thought you might hurt yourself or something."

She stood with her hand on her hips, skeptical, smiling. Dwight smiled sheepishly. "Okay, maybe a little bit afraid."

Just then, a strong wind buffeted the house, and the front door swung wide and then slammed shut again. He pulled her close. Through the sudden darkness, they made their way across the empty room. He reached for where he thought the knob should be but found nothing. The roar of the storm was muffled inside the closed house; thunder rumbled through the ancient, thick walls.

"Where's the door?" he whispered into her ear. "It was here a second ago." He smelled her shampoo, a soft, flowery invitation.

"I can't see anything," Dorothy said.

"Isn't this where the door was?" Dwight asked. Lightning flashed outside, but it did little to light up the interior. It cast fleeting, strange shadows on the walls and the floors in the eerie gray dimness.

Dorothy clenched her elbow. "This is not funny, Dwight. When this storm lets up, I am leaving this house and going home." She sniffled and wiped tears away with her sleeve. The storm raged outside, the house shook like it was going to fall down, and she was all alone with a boy she didn't know very well. For the first time in her life, she thought about what could happen in a situation like this. She was truly at his mercy, trapped in a house in a terrible storm.

Nothing about the scene was funny, but still she was embarrassed for the moment's weakness. She didn't want to be scared, she really didn't. It was all too crazy. A nice walk on an early fall day, the thrill of being with a boy she liked, all of it made her, well, even with the storm raging outside, even with the embarrassment of being scared after bragging about her bravery, even after all of it, she felt something inside of her, something weird. A tickle deep down, a happy tickle. Despite it all, she started to laugh.

At first, a small giggle bounced her shoulders. The next thing she knew, she was bent over at the waist laughing loudly.

Dwight stood back and smiled in the darkness. "You're a strange bird, aren't you? We're about to die and here you are laughing like you're at the county fair!" When she looked up at him, he stopped breathing. In the gray light, it was as if she had been transformed. Sure, she stood out that day among the other girls in the lunchroom, but that was kind of typical of love at first sight. He had seen it happen to other boys, some girl no one else would look twice at, and all of a sudden, some guy thinks she's the next Grace Kelly. But Dorothy, here, in this house, well, he was sure it was no trick of love at first sight. In the flashes of lightning, her face radiated health, energy, and, somehow, danger.

Dwight had never seen anything like that before, but he was sure he liked it.

He took both of Dorothy's hands in his. "There's a reason I wanted to bring you out here today," he said mysteriously.

Dorothy studied his face framed in the dreary light, the slope of his nose, the gentle, thin eyebrows. She watched as lightning flashed, thunder crashed. Hair framed his face as if it was a portrait painted by some surreal master. "We all have secrets," she replied, placing her index finger gently against his lips. She pulled him close to her, energy coursing through her body. This was a boy she could grow to be very fond of. Very fond, indeed.

She kissed him hard on his mouth. Their teeth clicked against each other as she tugged him across the room and down the hallway. She didn't want to know his "reason." She was afraid to hear it. She decided to change the subject, take control. Adrenaline coursed through her body, giving her courage she didn't believe in. "There's got to be another way out," she said between kisses.

Dwight heard her words as if from a great distance, but it didn't occur to him to say anything back. He had never kissed a girl before, and his emotions were running pretty high at that moment.

At the end of the hallway, Dorothy tried the door, but it was latched shut. Neither could make it budge. Dorothy pressed her ear against the wooden door and closed her eyes. She heard faint scratching sounds coming from within, like mice in the walls, but bigger, somehow. Cats, maybe. Her hand banged into another doorknob. She grasped it and turned it.

Dwight stepped back as the door swung open, feeling the damp and musty air rush at him. "That smells like a cellar," he said. "I don't think—"

Dorothy pulled him forward into the darkness. She placed his hand on the railing, and together they walked into the darkness and silence of the underground.

"Why—?"

"Shh," she hissed at him. "There's got to be a door out from the cellar, right? Or did you want to go upstairs?"

Dwight swallowed hard and followed her down. She was not the girl he thought she was, not the shy, submissive type. But this new adventure, the fear and thrill they were sharing, that was enough to keep him going. Man, if every day with Dorothy was like this, he'd have the most exciting life Kaukauna had ever seen.

She stopped when they reached the hard dirt floor. Dwight kept waiting for his eyes to adjust, but there was no light at all for them to adjust to. The air was warm and damp, the sound of the storm above them distant and muffled.

"Now we wait for lightning to show us where the cellar door is," Dorothy said. There was something different about her voice now, Dwight thought. Something confident, older. He squeezed her hand once, hoping she would return the squeeze just like his mother used to. Instead, he felt her hand drop away. He heard her walking away from him into the darkness.

Then all was silent. He tried not to breathe.

Dorothy wasn't sure where she had gotten all the confidence she had found there in that house. Something about it seemed so familiar, so easy, so much like, well, home, that she felt like there was nothing to be afraid of. She groped at the air in front of her and took small steps toward what she hoped would be the steps up to the door that led outside, but if she had to search a little bit, that was okay, too. In the silence, strange thoughts muddled with hers, thoughts of this house in happier days, a family living here, working here. But why should it be abandoned like this? Who would just leave a farm to get all overgrown, to watch a perfectly good house collapse in disrepair? None of it made any sense.

"Dwight? Are you still there?" she asked tentatively. "I could sure use a good laugh right now. Dwight?" But there came only silence from the darkness.

She stopped and turned her head back the way she had come. "Did you find the way out?" she whispered. "No fair not talking to me. I'm getting all spooked." She found him again in the blackness, found his hand at his side. It was cold, limp. "No fair not talking to me. Hey, you said you had a reason for bringing me here. I love secrets," she said bravely. "Tell me. Please."

Dwight had never been so afraid in his life, but he wanted his voice to sound confident. He took a deep breath and searched for something, anything to say. "I— well, it's just that I, well, I never kissed a girl before." The truth was hollow, hard, and he couldn't say it. For a moment it seemed as if another person, not himself, had made it all up. The thought of lying to Dorothy just to get her alone like that—Dwight just couldn't believe what his own imagination had cooked up. Dwight closed his eyes and flexed his fists closed and open, praying she would believe him. "I was worried, well, I was worried you'd be disappointed."

Dorothy ran her fingers through his hair and pulled his head close to hers. "Disappointed? Don't be silly. I think it's a fine thing. It makes you perfect. Quite perfect."

She pressed her lips to his, and Dwight could taste the cellar somehow, as if it had gotten into her mouth. He wanted to pull away, but how can you tell a girl you are kissing that she has bad breath? He was enough of a gentleman to know that was not the thing to do.

Dorothy pulled away and took his hand, guided him across the rough floor of the cellar. She said, "Do you wonder what happened to the people in this house? I mean the ones who lived here, where they went, why they moved?"

In the black, a tiny, yellow glow.

Dwight blinked hard, assumed it was a trick of his eyes, but there it remained.

An outline on the floor, long and thin. A faint glow in an otherwise black space, yellow, pale.

Another beside it.

Several small ones, too.

"Do you see that?" he gasped.

"Do you?" she replied.

"I don't know. I don't know," he stammered. "What is it?" Dwight wanted to move. He tried to move. But those glowing shapes on the floor somehow held him in place. "Let's get out of here, Dorothy. No fooling now. I really...."

Dorothy moved behind him, wrapped her arms around his waist.

Not an embrace.

Not at all.

More like being tied up.

Tied to the floor.

In the cellar of this house.

Tied to the floor to die.

"I told you we all have secrets," she cooed in his ear, her voice different, soothing, and distant.

Dwight tried to speak, but no words came out of his mouth. He struggled against her arms, tried to pull free. Please, he wanted to say. Please let me go. No words came out.

Her voice was otherworldly, weak, as if arriving to his ears from across a great distance. It was Dorothy's voice, but then again, it wasn't. It seemed to come not just from her but from all around him, from the air itself. "Many years ago, my family and I lived here. We'd come to Kaukauna to open a green grocery for the papermakers at the Thilmany Mill. We had only just arrived. Only a few people even knew we had moved into this strange, abandoned house way out here in the woods. On a stormy fall day like today, a band of thieves locked us down here, took everything we owned. It took them a week to do it. The whole time, thunder and lightning, hail the size of apples, just like today. We heard them up there drinking and fighting, spoiling our house. It was awful. They banged on the door at all hours, promising they'd come down to kill us as soon as they were done."

Dwight stood transfixed by her words and by what he saw there at his feet. Three shadows lined up on the floor, but not shadows, since all around them was darkness and they themselves cast only a faint light. The absence of a shadow. The absence of darkness. Three of them, two long and one tiny. A family of black shapes. He tried to speak, tried to move, but still could not.

"My parents—there they rest, uneasy, their spirits trapped in this place. And my—" her voice caught. Dwight felt her body shudder, as if she were sobbing silently. "—my brother, there. Oh, James. Only six years old." Dorothy's voice laughed. "And such a funny little boy, too."

She took Dwight by his shoulders and turned him. In the faint light, Dwight saw Dorothy's face transformed into something otherworldly. The face he first saw in the lunchroom that day, the face that had captivated him, had been magnified somehow, made beautiful and terrible in the yellow glow.

She pressed her fingers to his lips and whispered, "They did come downstairs, the whole stinking mob of them. My father met them at the bottom step with a hunk of firewood, but one of the thieves shot him in the leg. I never saw so much blood." She paused and looked away. "I said we all have secrets. Want to hear mine?"

Dwight stared at her wide-eyed. This was all too much. He tore his arms free of her and staggered to the stairs, took two at a time to the top. He fully intended to run, to flee from this house, but he stopped and turned, peered into the darkness below.

Then, from deep within the cellar, he heard a faint voice call to him, "Please."

He sagged, knew what he had to do. He grasped the rail and, like a man walking to the gallows, he descended the stairs. He had brought Dorothy here. He was responsible for her.

He reached her side—this transformed girl, the radiant beauty—and swallowed hard. He pushed the hair back from her cheek. "I'm sorry for running away. Tell me whatever you want."

Dorothy sighed. "The thieves said they'd let my family go if they could take me. They wanted me, I don't know why, those men. My father refused, stood there bravely on one leg. He hit one so hard in the head that they had to drag him up the stairs."

"Later that day, they shot my father in his other leg, told him he'd never walk again, and made him weep in agony. They beat my mother in front of me, breaking her arm. She couldn't speak after that, just held her head and moaned. I kicked and screamed, refusing to go with them."

Dwight didn't understand any of it, but he nodded gravely and whispered, "That's terrible." He wanted to help. He just couldn't figure out how.

Dorothy continued, "My father said crazy things, his mind ruined by losing all that blood," she pointed to the yellow shapes on the floor. "There he is now. Oh, father! And my mother hunched over him, her pain unbearable, clinging to him and to James." She gestured at the floor of the cellar. "I was right here. They didn't touch me."

Dwight said, "But there wasn't anything you could have done about it. Those thieves are to blame." He tried to pull her closer, to console her, but she pulled away angrily. "No!" she hissed. "You don't understand."

Dorothy frowned in concentration, as if trying to gather the courage to speak. She turned to Dwight, tears welling up in her eyes. "They said they were coming for me next. They said they'd kill us all." She buried her face in Dwight's shoulder and clenched her eyes shut. "I knew where we kept the coyote poison. I mixed the poison with water," she held her hands in front of her, pouring one imaginary bottle into another.

Dwight stood taller. "You killed those cowards?" he asked.

Dorothy spun and faced him, an anguished look in her eyes.

"I don't understand," Dwight whispered.

"Don't you see? It wasn't those men, they didn't kill my family," she sobbed. "It was me. I gave it to my father as he slept. Then I did the same to my mother and brother. I killed them before those men could come back down to do their worst. But when the time came for me to take my own dose, I just couldn't. I held it for hours right here, held it so close to my lips I could almost taste it. But I couldn't drink it. I didn't have the courage."

She raised her eyes to face him, questioning him, begging for some kind of answer.

Dwight stood, frozen in the moment. How could this be real? And yet there it all was. It all made a kind of tangled-up sense.

She continued, "I waited down there in the cellar all night. Nothing but silence upstairs. A day passed, then two. The bodies of my family... I had to escape no matter what the cost. I kicked down the door. The house was empty. The thieves were gone."

Dorothy collapsed to the cellar floor in tears. Dwight cradled her limp body, stroked her head in his lap. "It's all over now," he said softly.

"I buried them down here under the cellar floor," Dorothy said dreamily. "I locked the doors and then ran as far as I could. I went to California, I think. Sunshine and beauty all around. I think I was there. I think I had a life there, but all the time, my world was back here, in this cellar." She looked up at Dwight in wonder. A shaft of sunlight cut through a gap in the foundation, illuminated her face. "I think I died. I think I was an old woman, sad and alone. I don't think I had a good life. Or was it a dream? How is it I am back here now?"

Dwight's head spun. "Your name is Dorothy. You just moved to Kaukauna, Wisconsin, to start senior year. It is October 1960," he smiled through tears. "And you're a really great kisser!"

Dorothy laughed, her face for a moment just as it was when Dwight first saw her across the crowded lunchroom. She closed her eyes. "I need you to answer me." Dorothy swallowed, clenched her teeth, and breathed in deeply. "I need you to answer me very seriously. I need an honest answer. Okay? Can you do that for me?"

Dwight nodded gravely.

Dorothy held both of his hands tightly. "Did I do the right thing? I didn't know they were gone. I could have saved them all. I tried to do the right thing. I really tried. Oh, please tell me. Did I do the right thing?"

Dwight pulled her close. "Absolutely," he whispered. "You were brave and true. Courage like no one I have ever heard of. You did the right thing."

Dorothy opened her eyes wide in surprise as if that was not the answer she had expected. "I did the right thing," she whispered, surprised to hear those words coming from her mouth. She said it again, marveling at how the words felt as she said them.

In his arms, Dorothy smiled and began to glow like the others, a yellow radiance permeating the room, clearing the air as if a storm had passed, the sweet scent of autumn leaves on a gentle breeze.

Dwight held her tight, whispering into her ear, "You did the right thing."

The strange, yellow shape left her body, floated in the air above them, and swirled through the room, catching up the others in a dance of spirits freed from this earthly trap. Four spirits—a family reunion—darted this way and that through the cellar, into every crevice, over and around every rafter. One by one, the yellow shapes blazed upward through the rafters and up the stairwell, as if taking back their house after all these years. Soon they returned to the cellar, the four yellow shapes, swirled closely around Dorothy and Dwight, raising the hair on the backs of their necks, and then the pale-yellow shapes vanished through the gaps in the foundation and into the evening light.

There below, only the flesh and blood Dorothy remained. She sighed weakly and sagged into Dwight's arms.

All was as it had been. The boy and girl sat in the cellar of the abandoned old house, smelling the ordinary dirt and the remnants of the passing rain.

In silence, they climbed the stairs. They walked down the hallway and out onto the porch into the bright sunshine that angled in under the receding dark clouds. They walked hand in hand together through the forest downhill toward the river. Then they stopped and looked back at the old house.

After a long time, Dorothy whispered, "I felt everything the girl said. I lived her whole life as she told it. I felt it all. I felt what it was like to be alone, terrified of being close to anyone for fear of losing them." She turned to face Dwight, the boy she had met in the lunchroom, the boy she had walked with to this spooky, abandoned house, the boy who stayed with her when he could have run, when he could have looked out only for himself, when he could have run out on her. But in his eyes at that moment, she knew that she was where she belonged.

"Oh, it was terrible, horrible being alone like that. Nothing but regret." She raised her chin. "I don't want that for my life." She reached out and took his hand in hers. "I don't want that for you, either," she said.

She pulled Dwight close. They hugged each other as the sun set, as the gentle breeze stirred drops loose from the brightly colored leaves above that tickled their faces.

For a long time, Dwight held her silently. But then, all things considered, he couldn't help laughing. "What's so funny?" Dorothy asked.

"I was just thinking, how are we going to top this date? I mean, it's not like we can just go to the movies and pretend this never happened."

She pulled him close. "I have a few ideas..." They kissed right there at the edge of the clearing in the fading daylight.

THE BROTHER OF THE BRIDE

Boaters on Lake Winnebago in the mid-summer twilight report the voice of a young man calling for help in the gloomy mist just east of Oshkosh. Searches reveal nothing, even when the police have been called. There is a story that might explain the voice, however. On a summer's day in 1918, a young man and his new brother-in-law went fishing and found themselves surprised by a fast-moving squall. Their boat capsized, and the two men tried to hold on, but the young man's grip slipped, and he drowned. The brother-in-law swam for shore and was rescued. The rumor at the time, however, said that the man objected to his sister's choice of a husband and took the groom out onto the lake for a man-to-man talk. The discussion got heated, and the brother-in-law murdered the groom. The strange thing is that the voice reported out in the mist on the lake whose source has never been found, cries not for help but instead shouts a single word again and again in the misty darkness: "Don't!"

FIND A PLACE LIKE THIS

Marnie missed the low bar, and her coach missed the catch. Face-planted onto the floor. Padded, with springs under the pads, but wow, that hurt.

Knocked the life right out of her.

She was thirteen, long past the time when any natural gymnastics talent might reveal itself. She started off at five years old, hurtling through the air into the foam block pits with the best of them, laughing and smiling every day. Years passed, and now her mother seemed to want it more than she did. Her mom researched college programs, summer camps, private coaches—anything and everything possible. Marnie didn't want to disappoint her mom, but getting smashed in the face was also a bit of a disappointment. She wished that somebody would be honest with her and tell her that Marnie was a nice kid who should find some other way to spend her time.

A thin line of blood appeared on her index finger when she wiped her nose. That was her ticket out of there. "Hey, coach," Marnie said.

"Go clean yourself up," is all she said.

She walked out of the gym and down the hall to the locker room. Inside, she dabbed at her nose with a tissue, but the blood was mixed with sweat and looked to be slowing down to nothing. She still felt the impact with the mat and could see the faint pink blotch that stretched from ear to ear. Her back hurt, her knees hurt, her hips hurt, her shoulders hurt—all the time, everything hurt. She knew she had probably a half hour more in practice, but she just couldn't face it. Her friends were doing things together, watching tv, sitting at home—just doing whatever they wanted to. And here she was all afternoon after school, every day after school, pounding her body into pulp.

Her head still rang with the impact. Unless she kept her head still, the room spun slowly around her.

There were only a few younger girls in the locker room, and she walked with purpose past them to her own locker. She put on her shorts and jacket and slipped out the door at the end of the hall—on the other end of the building from the gymnastics room—and into the trees behind the building next to a row of townhouses. The roar of the cars on the highway behind sounded to Marnie like running water.

She stepped lightly through the tall grass and let the summer leaves brush past her face. She trained indoors during the summer with no air conditioning, and so anywhere outside felt cool and pleasant. Her mother wasn't due for a while, and so she walked down the street. She thought about breathing and, for a moment, forgot how to do it. She took in a deep breath through her mouth and then let it out slowly, expecting to see winter's cloud of vapor before remembering the season. She laughed and then coughed weakly.

Loud bangs and the roar of engines drew her to the old, white, one-story, windowless building down the block. *Americanos*, the side of the building said, but there was never anyone there.

Until today.

Now there were trucks and bulldozers and a temporary chain-link fence around the whole property. Half of the building was already gone into a pile of rubble that a big, yellow machine was scooping up and dropping into a dump truck. Marnie laced her fingers through the fence to balance herself. The sun seemed especially strong this afternoon.

She'd never seen a building demolished before. She imagined being inside while it was happening. She imagined her own house if they came in the middle of the night. What if her roof just fell down like that one just did? How could she stop it? She'd run to the window, but what if the workers didn't hear her? And her parents downstairs? They'd probably escape. They'd probably be out on the front lawn and not remember about her until it was too late. Mom would probably grab some of my trophies and forget about me.

The noise hurt her teeth.

The bright sunshine, too.

"This was a magical place," a voice said.

Marnie turned to see an old woman standing next to her. She regarded the scene with sadness in her eyes and clenched her teeth.

Marnie didn't say anything.

Instead, she looked at her gymnastics school where the doors were open, and the classes continued. Girls flung themselves in all directions, a daily routine Marnie knew well but that seemed distant at that moment, as if someone else had done the things she did, someone else had been taking gymnastics classes all these years.

Mixed in with the roar of the trucks and the splintering of wood was a new sound. It buzzed like a mid-summer field of insects or the crackle of electricity. She pressed the palms of her hands against her eyes.

"I feel the same way," the old woman said. Her voice sounded faint and distant. "Do you know what this place was?"

Marnie felt dizzy and sick. She clenched her eyes shut as the world spun around her. She felt the old woman's hand touch hers. It was soft and warm. "My name is Michelle. Like the song."

Marnie opened her eyes again and blinked. The sky, so sunny before, had grown overcast. The trucks had vanished. The building, impossibly, stood intact and freshly painted.

"Come on, Shelly!" the boy shouted. He walked a few steps ahead of her into the parking lot that was filled with antique cars. He was dressed in a flamboyant suit of red and white. He wore a tall hat and carried what looked like an instrument case. "We'll be late!"

There was no more fence, and Marnie's hands were cold all of a sudden. She took a deep breath. She touched the tip of her nose but found no blood there. She didn't remember changing her clothes, but she was wearing a red dress with white flowers embroidered onto the hems and a white bow around her neck.

"Come on!" the boy shouted.

"Americanos" was emblazoned on the side of the building, and crowds of people entered through the front door. It was decorated with a large wreath festooned with brightly colored ribbons. For a moment, Marnie lost sight of the boy. Inside smelled like cinnamon, pine trees, and chocolate. Chairs were set up in long rows in the big room. At the end of the room was a stage where kids in uniforms were setting up music stands.

Marnie moved off to the side of the room to look for the boy. Up on stage were others dressed like him with their uniforms and horns. Colors shifted, and a breeze picked up. Heat and then cold washed over her. Soon the audience settled into their seats, rows on rows of the eager faces of parents, grandparents, and friends. Marnie recognized the scene from gymnastics.

But there was a difference here.

At her meets, parents shouted encouragement and berated the judges. Their faces reflected tension, disappointment, and anger, mostly. That, and boredom.

Here, things were different, and it wasn't just the free hot chocolate they were handing out, either. The audience looked... happy. The kids on stage were milling about getting ready, and they looked happy, too.

Soon they were seated, as well, and the stage lights came on. The band leader came out, and they played a tuning note. They started soft and quiet with "Silent Night," "Away in a Manger," "Oh, Come All Ye Faithful," and soon they were off in a mad dash through "Jingle Bells," "The Twelve Days of Christmas," "Rudolph the Red-Nosed Reindeer," and a rousing rendition of "All I Want for Christmas Is My Two Front Teeth."

The boy Marnie met played the trumpet, and she imagined that he could see her there in the shadows at the back of the room. It did seem as if he was staring at her the entire time.

All the songs had a kind of Spanish flair to them, with the drummers leading the way with the Latin beat. They looked like they were having so much fun up there, all raising their arms in unison before landing on the beat with a crash. The band had funny choreography, and the band leader told some corny jokes along the way, too. The crowd sang along, and the band ate it all up.

By the time they were finished, everyone was standing up and dancing right there at their seats. It was the most joyful moment—parents and kids and Christmas time and just pure fun. The music was amazing and took a ton of practice, she knew, but the show was pure magic.

Even after it was over, the crowd stayed and ate cookies and chatted. The musicians came out to hugs and smiles with their families. And suddenly the boy was in front of Marnie, a look of uncertainty on his face. "What did you think?" he asked timidly.

Marnie put her hands on his shoulders. "It was the most wonderful thing I've ever seen!" she gushed.

he said. "You should join! They just started letting girls play, too!"

"I saw! Some on the drums, even. But how do you even join something like this? I don't know how to play anything."

The boy replied, "You must know something, right? Piano lessons?"

Marnie shook her head.

"Choir? Nothing? No matter. I have a great teacher here, and we can be in the trumpet section together!"

Marnie felt lighter than air. The room around her buzzed with excitement and energy. The boy stood close to her, and she could smell his hair gel, and the Christmas lights reflected in his eyes. "Actually, those drums look like a lot of fun to me."

The boy smiled. "Anything you want! This place is amazing. Want to meet the drum teacher? He's right over there."

The buzzing filled the room. The boy tried to pull her by the sleeve through the crowd, but she stopped and pressed her hands to her ears. "Are you—"

"—okay?" the old woman asked. Through the mist, Marnie could see the sky framing the woman's concerned face. It was familiar somehow, that face. Gone was the crowd and the room and the winter. Bright sun and heat pressed down on her.

"Stay here, and I'll get help," the old woman said.

Marnie was lying down, and the ground felt like a good place to be. As she breathed, it was as if the world spun below her, as if she was chasing the air to catch her breath.

The boy stood before her again. "I'm sorry you're not feeling well," he said.

"Who are you?" she asked.

"I'm just a guy. I could be anyone."

She tried to smile. Her head hurt.

"What?" she whispered. It was all a dream, right? Like she was watching a movie.

Two men stood above her. One blocked the sun. "What's your name?" one of them asked.

"Are you the drum teacher?" Marnie responded dreamily.

The boy said, "I need to go now, I think. Remember this place. We had fun here. Find a place like this for yourself."

"I don't know how to play," Marnie said.

"The world is music," he replied. "Don't just listen. Play!" His image grew brighter and faded to yellow and blue.

"What's your name?" a different woman asked.

Marnie's head swirled. Too many voices. Too many people asking her questions, telling her what to do. Her eyes were closed, but she felt the warmth of the sun on her face, and a hand on her cheek. "My name is Shelly," she whispered to the boy.

"We're going to take good care of you, Shelly," a woman's voice said

The image of the clubhouse faded, the colorful lights, the wisps of snow falling, the sharp chill in the air. The boy stood in the doorway framed by bright lights. He put a hand over his heart. "Merry Christmas," she shouted.

"I guess it's Christmas somewhere, right?" the woman's voice said lightly. Marnie caught a glimpse of herself being lifted into the ambulance. "Climb right up here," the voice said. Someone new took her hand.

"I'm right here," Marnie's mother said. "I am right here."

Marnie opened her eyes. "I want to learn to play the drums," she said.

THE CHELSEA PHONE

During the deluge, I found shelter in the Fox Cities Mall where I used to work. In the food court, rain came right through the vaulted ceiling onto people eating pizza and terrible Chinese food. Nobody but me seemed to notice. I bought bottled water at the CVS and recognized the irony. Still soaked, I sat alone in the new octoplex, and the lights went down. I watched a New York City film about outdoor art-object tables from the 1970s with the Checkers and the muscle cars in the background as plain as the sun. I rode a glass-top coffee table through the closing credits down the Central Park transverse. I glided down 7th Avenue back when it was still two ways, down the long hill to the Village past factories and then farms. At the bottom of the hill, when the road disappeared, there were people at the edge of the forest at the end of 7th Avenue riding small bicycles in circles, racing to see who was faster. Night was coming, and the final heats were set for the next morning. I slipped through the rope defining the course and rode my glass-top coffee table past the bikes and into the wilderness. I rode up the hill past huge furry rodents. A saber-toothed groundhog ran ahead of me into the brush. Birds and snakes stared at me from the tops of apple trees until I came upon a falling-down mansion that looked a lot like my sister-in-law's house at Lake Geneva. The lights were on; I saw her standing backlit on the porch. She waved me over, agitated, shouting something I could not understand. On the shallow lake where I grew up, I saw my brother Nate, who lives now in Manhattan, as a child in a gray wood rowboat out on the lake. He waved back to me. The next second, the rowboat overturned, and he was in the water, flailing and sputtering, drowning. He sank below the surface. I flew down the hill to the dock on my glass tabletop and jumped into the lake. Near the foundering rowboat, I found him; my glass tabletop sunk into the green shadows. I pulled his lifeless body up onto the shore and flipped him onto his back. Nate was now a small orange inflatable water toy. In fact, he was the smiley squirt ball I bought for my niece last summer. I had just taken CPR; it was fresh in my mind. I found the purple mouth that had been stamped onto the smiley squirt ball and did mouth-to-mouth. He had no chest, no thorax at all, and so I tried to revive him with just rescue breathing. I blew in air and squeezed out water simulating respiration. But his plastic form lost shape. It no longer flexed or held the pressure; the smile stamped onto the plastic shriveled and warped. My brother Nate was dead. I told myself I forced myself awake from the dream, decided to call him even at this early morning hour. In the next room, my own little daughter began to cry. I imagined her having the same dream and mourning the death of her uncle she had barely met, feeling his presence like a soft breeze that stirs the curtains, a sagging diaper, or a tooth coming in. I pulled the covers over my head, and I didn't move. My daughter's screams intensified. My wife rose and trudged off down the hall to soothe her. I laid awake waiting for the sun to rise in our now-silent house. It hadn't yet, but in my mind, I heard the Chelsea phone ringing.

THE USS *SCORPION*, LOST WITH ALL HANDS

Gray clouds rolled in from the north across Lake Winnebago and cast the steely May waters into a turmoil. White caps fizzed and bubbled in all directions as Steve, a fifteen-year-old boy, struggled with the sail on the little boat. The sun had fallen behind the roiling clouds in the west, leaving him out in the middle of Lake Winnebago, a mile from shore, trying to tack across a stiff breeze and, maybe soon, a storm, too. To the west, the lights of Neenah, his hometown, flickered in the gathering twilight but soon became fuzzy in the fog that rode the advancing bank of clouds.

"Captain's log, supplemental. A routine star-mapping assignment." He pulled on the boom line. "I can still tack my way there," Steve said nervously to himself. "No problem, even if it takes all night." He was wiry and strong and thought himself an experienced sailor. So, when he "borrowed" the little sailboat from the marina that afternoon, he thought he'd be clean out of sight and gone before anyone would notice. Not that he'd get into trouble. He was special, and he made it work to his advantage. Steal a boat? Puppy dog eyes and wipe away a tear. No problem, poor kid. Take the boat anytime you want.

He'd be needed down in Florida for real space travel, Steve thought. That's where I need to be. Not here where all they can talk about is bad news. July for Apollo 11. Two months to get there. At maximum warp, it was possible. Definitely. If they can make it to the moon, I can make it to Florida.

As the sky darkened, however, he was still having trouble tacking the boat south and across the wind when the first stinging, icy drops of rain pelted him.

The little boat struggled to stay pointed in any one direction as waves crested over the bow and water sloshed around the boy's ankles. Steve let the boom swing port and starboard, trying to get everything heading in the right direction, but no matter what he tried, the boat's prow kept turning east, pushed irresistibly by the wind toward the sparsely settled eastern shore of the lake. Waves broke over the gunwales, and the little boat was in danger of getting swamped.

Again and again, Steve filled an empty coffee can and dumped it over the side. He tried to bail and till at the same time, but neither was having much of an effect. With the cresting waves and the steady rain, he could barely keep up. Soon, Steve abandoned the sail altogether and grabbed another rusty coffee can and bailed with two hands. The little sailboat spun and drifted where the wind pushed it while the shivering, soaked boy frantically dumped water over the side.

Steve stopped for a moment and scanned the wooded shoreline. Neenah was nowhere in sight. And the cold wind now stung him, blasted through his wet clothes and through his skin. He opened his knapsack, unfolded the three shirts he brought with him, and put them on. He stuck socks on his hands for warmth, too, but none of that helped. He was cold and getting colder. If he couldn't get turned in the right direction soon, and if the temperature kept dropping, he might end up in Fond du Lac at the business end of an iceberg.

That thought made him laugh. "Ay, sir. Just getting my space legs under me," Steve lied to himself. He was getting good at lying to himself these days. "All part of sailing. We'll be out of the ion storm any minute now and on our way again."

Steve stopped bailing and hunched over for warmth. He was somewhere out in the middle of the lake now. He bent forward, closed his eyes, and focused on the sound of the wind hissing through the mast lines. But just as soon as it had blown up, the wind stopped. No more raindrops fell, either. It had all stopped. He had seen that before here in Wisconsin: a strong front blows through, leaving calm behind it. The trouble here was no longer the rain but the cold. The northwest wind had brought with it icy air. The rain had stopped, sure, but on this May afternoon, Steve could swear he smelled snow in the air.

He shook out his wet ball cap. If he could only stop shivering. His light spring clothes were soaked through. He hadn't planned on a survival mission in arctic temperatures, just an escape from home and the bad news that waited there. If he could outrun the news, travel at warp speed, maybe he could keep it all from happening.

The wind and rain were bad enough, but he preferred them to what he now faced: a dead calm and mounting cold. Steve searched all around him in the failing light. Except for the water immediately nearby, he could see nothing but a blank wall of gray as if he had been scooped out like ice cream from the world.

"Now what do we do?" Steve fingered the zipper on his jacket. He checked the knots on the sail rigging. He didn't want to have to explain himself, even if it was to himself. He hid from the truth like that. But then he remembered something his older brother Frank had told him the last time he was home. How long ago was it, two years now? A submarine crewman, out on some secret missions in the world, he just didn't have time to come home much. And Steve didn't blame Frank one bit. Why would anyone want to come home to a dump like Neenah when they were out seeing the world, going where no man has gone before?

What was it that Frank had told him? Take stock of the situation. Be honest. Find the things you can control and then make them work for you.

"It looks like the wind has died down a little bit, but we do need a little bit of wind to get us moving again... I ate plenty today, and I have food for a few days packed... I know the shore is around here someplace, and any dry land is better than being out here, so if I pick a direction, I'll get where I'm going..."

As he spoke, the last remaining light of day dwindled. Darkness pressed in on him from every direction.

And soon even the darkness was gone. It was like dying, Steve thought. "Lake Winnebago. The final frontier."

He pulled the collar of his jacket up over his head. He had never liked the cold, even after spending all his winters in a frigid northern outpost. Neenah was the kind of remote ice planet that Captain Kirk would find, conquer, and abandon in an hour. Not live there forever and watch his life disappear into nothingness or, even worse, a pity job at a paper mill.

"Captain's log, star date 1672 point 1," Steve flipped open his hand and spoke into his palm. "Stranded on the surface of Alpha 177. Tell Spock it's fine if the transporter duplicates things; I am willing to live with the evil blanket." Sometimes the show bugged him. Not usually, but sometimes. "I'll let Sulu have the good-natured, gentle blanket, if that's what worries you, Spock. Get the replicators working overtime here. Start beaming down blankets! And I'll drink the evil hot chocolate, too."

Steve sat back against the gunwale; his arms folded across his chest. He could hear the lake whisper beneath him, could even hear the distant whir of the mills on some shore. Menasha? Oshkosh? Where were they coming from? He couldn't tell. And the sky above, the endless expanse of blackness and stars up there—the moon itself—was all obscured by the black mist that hung in the air all around him. Just get across this lake, he thought to himself. Once I get across and no one knows me, I can make good time hitching down to the Cape. "Long past time to get my life going," Steve hummed to himself. "The news just pushed me where I wanted to go."

He squinted. The mist had changed somehow. It carried a faint, deep red, as if he had rubbed his eyes too hard, or shined a flashlight through the thin skin of his fingertips. Then he heard something strange and sat up tall, his ears alert.

A hissing, or a gentle whoosh. It could have been a sound from the shore or from another boat. "Lieutenant, open a channel. This is Captain Steven T. van Dyke of the USS *Enterprise*. We are on a peaceful mission. Please respond."

And then he saw it. In the fog ahead of him, the water glowed red as if lit from below. Steve whispered, "Spock, analysis." He stared intently into the darkness.

The water churned frothy, bubbles rising rapidly to the surface, all bloody in color as if the earth itself had been wounded. "Pure energy," Steve whispered. "Like nothing we've encountered before."

He remembered the filmstrip from science class on luminescent fish of the deep ocean and how they'd use light to lure their prey. Filmstrips were his favorite. The dark room, no one staring at him, no one making fun. Just the big world out there flickering in the dark. Not real like *Star Trek*, but still better than stupid school.

Steve leaned over the side of the sailboat and gazed into the water. The usual brown murk of the lake glowed red behind him, but it wasn't moving like a school of fish. The light seemed to be coming from one place, as if someone had a powerful red lamp deep down there.

As he watched, the bubbles intensified, the red light illuminating the misty air around him like fire. Suddenly, the water below him roared to life, and the red glow enveloped his little boat. He rocked from side to side as the water roiled beneath him. The red light had been below him. Now it was at water level. Then above him. A wall of blackness filled his vision, rain clattered down on him from above. It was all he could do to keep his little boat from flipping over.

And then, bathed in the glow of the red light, the lake calmed down again. The bubbles and frothing stopped. An island of blackness rose, a steep, sheer cliff of glistening metal glowed in the strange red light. Steve froze in terror.

The little sailboat bobbed in the turgid water and banged up against something hard. Steve reached out for it and touched cold metal. "A ship!" he whispered. "How could it be?"

Something heavy scraped above him, out of sight, followed by a loud clank of metal on metal. "A submarine!" he whispered.

Just then, one end of a heavy rope landed with a thud inside his little sailboat.

The other end snaked up the blank, black side of the mysterious ship.

For a moment, Steve couldn't breathe, it was all so fantastic. Alone in the boat, he wondered what he should do next. A captain goes down with his ship. Captain Kirk would never abandon the *Enterprise* or his five-year mission. Steve clung to the side of the little sailboat and imagined what his father might say when he told him he had stolen and then lost somebody's boat. And this submarine? How would anybody believe that? But if he died out there, his father might be mad, too. Steve smiled. There was no way his father would not be mad about this. So why not abandon ship?

He took the rope in his hands and felt its weight. It would certainly hold him. He stood in his little boat and tugged on the rope. He could climb that, no problem. He looked down at his little boat that sparkled in the red glow. "Hey, boat, try to make it back to the marina by dawn, okay? You remember the way, right?"

And with that, Steve climbed the rope, higher and higher, until he reached the deck. He climbed the ladder up the outside of the sub's sail. The main hatch was open, and he climbed down the interior ladder to the empty and dim submarine control room. Above him, the hatch clanked shut, locking out the nighttime cold, locking him inside.

From deep inside the sub, steam hissed, and valves clanked, as if the whole thing were alive somehow and was digesting a meal of Steve. He looked all around at the various gauges and lamps that flashed and spun, wondering what it all meant. He thought about Frank's advice. He knew that there were some things he could still control, even in this weird situation.

But the loud bang of a hatch closing somewhere in the humid distance brought him back to reality. Yes, something he could control. Ghosts on a ghost submarine? Likely, no.

Steve stepped away from the forward hatchway. He frowned and imagined what might come through that door. The sub had rescued him, it is true. So maybe they're friendly. But who ever heard of a sub in Lake Winnebago? Maybe they're something else.

Klingons?

Romulans?

Something like that.

He tensed his fists, ready for battle.

The heavy black latch spun to release the hatchway door. Steve breathed deeply and raised his fists.

The door swung open and a man in a Navy uniform stood revealed in the opening. For a moment, Steve's eyes stopped on the uniform, the starched blue and white, the medals festooning the breast. Then he swung his head up higher.

A face he recognized.

His brother, Frank!

Steve leaped into Frank's arms with a whoop. Frank smiled and hugged him tight. "How are you, squirt?"

Steve sobbed into his brother's shoulder, "You're here! I knew you would be. They're all wrong, Dad and all of them," he croaked, a hard lump clogging his throat.

Frank laughed and tousled Steve's hair, "What's the idea of you, Mr. Knucklehead, out here in the middle of the lake about to get your ass frozen off?"

"I was—" Steve stammered. "I was running away." He hung his head, embarrassed, then his face brightened. "I was going to Cape Kennedy to watch the launch of the moon shot."

Frank looked at him quizzically and then nodded gravely. "And why were you running away?"

"Because they said, well, they said you weren't coming back. They said your boat sank."

Frank laughed. "Sank? Impossible. Who told you that?"

"Dad. All of them."

"And you believed them?"

Steve closed his eyes. His head hurt. Believed who? Yes, no, he didn't know anymore.

Frank looked at him closely. "You sure you want to run away?" He let his brother go. "I know you probably have a lot of questions. I don't have a lot of time. Believe me, I had to move mountains to sign this boat out for the night. So let me show you around a little bit. Sit right here," Frank said pointing at one of the seats along the hull that faced a dizzying array of gauges and switches. "Here is how you control the speed of the engines and the pitch of the diving planes. Here. Push her up to a quarter speed."

But how do we know where we're going?" Steve asked seriously. Frank leaned over him and pointed out what the various instruments did.

Steve tuned him out and shook his head. None of this is happening. None of it. He rubbed his eyes.

He felt a heavy hand land on his shoulder. He opened his eyes to see his older brother's energetic face beaming at him. "Time to bring us home, Captain."

Steve frowned. "Who? Me?"

Frank nodded sternly. "Orders, Captain?"

Steve nodded, deep in thought. "Please just take us home."

"Course, speed, and depth, sir?"

"Back to Neenah."

Frank smiled uneasily and leaned close to Steve. "You're not playing the game the right way, Steve. Come on. Believe it a little bit." He stepped back and lifted his chin. "Course, speed, and depth, sir?"

Steve hated being conned. He hated the feeling that someone was pulling something on him. It happened all the time at school. Recess, even the teachers sometimes. Frank, too? He hated being played for the fool.

Neenah was to the west, he knew that. He had sailed almost due east before he lost his bearings. The wind likely pushed him south. Steve cleared his throat, whispered uneasily. "Uh... course 300 degrees, one-quarter speed, dive to... Hey, is it possible to dive to ten feet? I mean, it's Lake Winnebago we're talking about."

Frank snapped, "Your orders, Captain?"

Steve smiled and said, "Helmsman, bring us around, course 300 degrees, three-quarter speed. Periscope depth."

Frank beamed. "Aye-aye, sir."

Frank leaped from station to station, and the ship came alive. Somewhere in the distance, engines rumbled to life. Steve felt the deck beneath his feet shift slightly, as if they were underway and picking up speed fast. He flicked switches and spun dials as if he were born for it.

Frank raised the periscope to Steve's eye level. Steve grabbed both handles and peered through the lenses. Outside, he saw nothing but darkness. The fog remained on the surface, and the lake was calm. Still, they made headway—he could feel it through his shoes. They'd reach some shore soon. He scanned ahead of him and off to the port and starboard, looking for lights, a town, anything. The ping of sonar brought him back to the interior of the sub. Frank pointed out the readings on a circular scope.

Back to the periscope. Out in the middle of the lake, this depth was no problem. Steve knew enough about the lake to know that near the shore; however, it was shallow and muddy. Perfect for mucking things up. And he had already done that enough for one day. But in all this thick fog, how could they see the shore before they ran aground?

Then he saw it. At first, he thought it might be just a trick of the twin periscope lenses. But there it was again. A faint white light. Steve knew exactly what it was, knew exactly where they were. And he was alarmed—he had to think fast.

"Full stop!" he shouted.

"Helm answering," Frank replied.

Steve pulled back from the periscope as he felt the ship slow down dramatically when Frank cut the engine. He noticed a compass mounted in the periscope, and in a second, he knew how to read it. "Surface running, helmsman. Change course. Heading..." Steve thought for a moment, did the calculation again to make sure of himself, checked the faint light in the periscope, the light at Lighthouse Park, right there in his hometown of Neenah, Wisconsin. He took a deep breath. "Heading 2-9-7. Take us home, Frank."

"Hey! You've got to call me helmsman or lieutenant or something."

Steve smiled. "Okay, Mr. Sulu. Bring us in slow and easy."

Frank leaned forward in his seat. "Aye, captain. Slow and easy."

Through the periscope, the lighthouse beamed its white light high above everything else, but soon the lights of Neenah materialized through the mist as if from a dream. His course was straight and true and brought him toward the opening of the channel just south of Doty Island. Most houses were dark; it must be after midnight, Steve thought. But the mills and the lights downtown shone brightly.

Through his feet, he felt the engines wind down to silence. He felt the sub decelerate and then drift. He pulled his eyes from the periscope to see Frank beaming at him.

"Are you home now for good?" Steve asked.

Frank smiled uneasily, then slowly shook his head. "But it's time for you to go home, little brother." He reached for the ladder that led up to the sail hatch where they had climbed in.

Steve studied his brother's face. "Aren't you coming, too? Dad's going to be mad if you don't."

Frank pulled Steve close and hugged him hard. "You tell Dad I always meant to come home. I didn't want to stay away for so long. Tell him I miss him."

Frank took hold of the cold metal ladder and climbed up through the narrow tube to the hatch. He spun the hatch open, and the night air pressed in on them from above.

He hopped down on the deck next to Steve. "There you go, Captain." In a daze, Steve climbed the ladder out onto the sail. The night had turned colder, and the lights of the Neenah marina flickered dimly in the mist.

Steve looked back down into the hatch. For a moment the world spun beneath him, and he grasped the rail for balance. The black circle at his feet yawned open, a mouth drawing him closer, darkness, a doomsday machine. "Frank!" Steve shouted. "Come up here right now!"

He wanted to reach his foot downward for that first step of the ladder. He wanted desperately to go back down there to join Frank no matter where he went. But if what those men said was true, then none of it was real. And how can anyone tell what's real and what's not?

"Frank!" Steve shouted. He wanted to leap back inside the sub, jump into the maw of the doomsday device, destroy it from within, but he couldn't get his feet to move. He felt cold tears running down his face. " "I'm a coward," he thought. " "He's right there, my own brother, and I'm too weak to save him."

He rocked back and forth at the rail at the top of the sub's towering sail. "There is no third planet," he whispered again and again. "You think I don't know that?"

Finally, he closed his eyes and let go. He fell backwards, away from the void, out into the darkness.

Somebody was shaking him gently awake. His mind cleared enough to hope it was Frank, but when he opened his eyes, he saw the concerned face of his father. The sky had brightened toward sunrise.

"Frank!" Steve sat up excitedly.

"No," his father whispered. "It's just me. I've been looking for you all night."

Steve struggled unsteadily to his feet. Water sloshed through his shoes as the little sailboat, moored securely at the marina, rocked from side to side. "He's here!" Steve shouted.

"I wish he was, too. Believe me," his father whispered. His father helped Steve onto the dock.

Steve looked around confused. "The *Scorpion* was here, right here. And Frank was, too."

Steve's father put his hands on Steve's shoulders. "You had a dream, son. That's all. You ran away and you've been out here all night. Too cold for your own good."

And some little thing came back to Steve... the black sedan in the driveway and the two Navy men who rang the front bell... the hushed conversation upstairs with Dad... Dad walking into the TV room just as Commodore Decker told Kirk and Spock that to save his crew he had transported all of them to the surface of the third planet in this system... and Kirk's reply...

Steve tried to shake out that dream in favor of the other one. He tried to make the choice that would save Frank. He knew that what you believed was important and how hard you believed it made the most difference.

No third planet...

You think I don't know that?

THE NIGHT THE WORLD ENDED ON DOTY ISLAND

Doty Island is filled with ghosts—and no wonder. It was the site of one of the most gruesome tragedies in state history. On a late summer night in 1888, at a Doty Island paper mill, a fire broke out in the boiler room. The whole neighborhood—several hundred, by some estimates—gathered outside to watch the spectacle. They crowded along the outer brick wall of the mill and tried for a glimpse at the inferno inside. Firefighters trained their water jets onto the heart of the blaze, but the mix of sudden cold and extreme hot set off a devastating explosion of the chemicals inside the mill. The massive brick and timber walls of the mill disintegrated and rocketed outward into the crowd while pieces of the shattered roof flew high into the air and crashed back down seconds later onto the shocked spectators. In the chaos, people dug through the rubble to save loved ones or wandered bleeding through the tumult.

The mill, of course, is long since gone, but the ghosts of that night live on. These days, after midnight on Doty Island, when the traffic thins and only the mill sounds hiss through the night air, faint, frantic voices of the long-dead can be heard calling unusual, antique names: Baltzur! Myron! August! Colly! The voices of the crushed and burned that blazing night still clamor for their loved ones; their spirits, confused and broken, wander the island in anguish and confusion.

Go ahead, try to find the source of those terrifying voices. You won't. Just stop for a while, listen, and remember the hot August night when the whole world exploded, and twenty citizens of Doty Island died.

THE NIGHT COCKEREL

The dream opens on a white sandy beach. Clear water. Completely colorless. The waves are smallish, like a harbor or bay, but the horizon is uniform and boundless. I stand at the water's edge, feeling the soft, warm water splashing rhythmically against my ankles. The near shore is filled with people, all wading silently like me. Strangely, it is almost dark, at least it seems near dusk. But the sun is directly overhead in the clear, dark blue sky. It can muster only about a moon's worth of light, however.

My wife is on a towel, ten feet from the water's edge. Her knees are up, and she is propped on her elbows. She is wearing the sun hat we bought when she was still in school, a good few years ago. The hat seems hardly necessary. She is waving toward me, silently, beckoning me. Becoming more insistent. Then she doubles up in pain, knees and feet toward her chest, chin to her breast. I run across the sand to her; it takes longer than I thought it would. By the time I arrive, she is surrounded by her old girl friends from high school and college, her mother, and her sister. I push my way through them and drop to my knees next to her.

"What's wrong?"

"It's time. It's time." She spits the words out through gritted teeth, and I am grabbed beneath the armpits by the other women. My wife screams, and I am spun out of the circle, back toward the water.

"Time for what?"

But suddenly I am back on the deserted, silent beach, my wife sleeping on the towel.

"Time for what?" I shake her awake.

"Time for a baby, beautiful. It's time. Let's go." She stands. From behind, she is as skinny as ever. She turns and begins to shake out her towel, smiling at me, her abdomen huge with a late-term pregnancy.

"What baby? Are you pregnant? Why didn't you tell me? How come I didn't know all this time?" I grab her by the arm, stopping her from gathering our things. "Are you in labor? Do we have a doctor? A midwife?" She laughs quietly and turns to walk up the beach carrying most of our things.

Now we are in my childhood bedroom. I am crouched atop my old wooden dresser, trying to get a better look at what is happening on the bed in the corner. My wife, surrounded by other women, writhes in pain, screaming for water (not for me), on her back, knees up, pressed to her chest, her chin buried into her breast. She is naked and sweating. Her friend from grade school sees me. She turns toward me, holding a towel soaked with blood, and tells me to go outside and throw it in the garbage. Her voice is calm, but it carries with it a tone of warning. Don't get too close to this, she seems to say. It is better if you stay away, she seems to say.

I wad the towel into a ball, trying to be of use, trying to puzzle out what is going on. I know the way to the garbage cans, of course, having grown up in this suburban house, and I turn left through the screen door. It is twilight, the air comfortable, the world silent.

Sitting perched on the old basketball backboard in our backyard is a huge gray shape. I stop, holding the bloody towel, to stare at this unexpected sight. It must be an owl of some sort—I should know the names of at least some owls, right—and just then it breaks into flight. It glides above the house, momentarily disappearing over the roof, only to return, wings spread wide and strong, talons unsheathed, to attack. I crouch next to the garbage can, using it as a shield. It comes at me, batting its wings at the last second to avoid crashing into my head. I feel its feathers sweep by me, and the firmness and fragility of its bones are combined with a good deal of weight.

I know for certain now that it is a gray owl. It turns in mid-air and comes down at me again, ready for the kill. I think calmly of the skull and bone-crushing power of those talons. I think of the flesh-ripping, knife-sharp beak. I know my bare arms will be injured badly, but I put them over my head anyway, trying to protect myself in any way I can.

The owl hits me with all of its force, pouncing on me, much heavier than I thought it might be. It hits my forearm first, both talons. She is quick, deliberate, and overwhelmingly powerful.

Female.

Hypnotic.

Female, I don't know how I know it.

I feel the weight of her daggers, I can feel the bones in my forearm, now so fragile, as they are about to be shattered.

The soft wing feathers sweep by my face, almost gently, as the owl tries to maintain its balance. Her talons do not break my skin, however. Not even close. Instead, I feel something more like a firm handshake than anything else. After a moment, the owl takes off again, big wings lifting it up and out to the backboard where she lands and sits, looking down at me. I get to my feet and dust myself off, still not trusting the owl, and hurry back to the door. I open it and go inside, closing it tight, sliding the deadbolt shut.

The bedroom crowd around my wife has thinned a bit and I recognize only a few of the ten or so women now in the room. I push past them to the bed. My wife is covered in sweat, still screaming, knees and chin to chest—now clearly in labor. I yell frantically, "Is there a doctor here? Are any of you doctors? Or midwives? Somebody get some help! She's going to die!" Strong arms pull me by one shoulder, spinning me away.

I turn, determined to get back to her side, when I see the other bed in the room. It is the one my little brother used to sleep on. The blue plain sheets—again, the same old ones—are disheveled as if someone had slept and had gotten up without making the bed again. On the bed sits the owl, staring at me. I am about to yell in alarm, but then I see the windows. They are open wide, screens and all. I look from the windows to the group of women, some of whom are now staring at me menacingly. The owl has lost interest in me. She has resumed digging and pulling at something under the sheets, using her claws to hold it down.

"There's a dangerous animal in here! Somebody help—let's get this out of here!" But nobody moves. I rush over to the bed and grab the sheets, intending to throw them over the owl, gather the bundle up in my arms.

And that's what I try to do. In the process, however, I expose what it was that the owl was tearing at. A small, brown, curly-haired child, about one year old, lies dead in my brother's bed, naked, with small rips and tears on its face and chest. The owl had just begun to eat.

I throw the sheet with the owl inside out the window.

"There's a baby here! That owl killed a baby! Whose baby is this? We've got to find out!" I don't touch the child. I look closely, though. Its eyes are open, arms out to either side, surrendering. Small pieces of flesh hang in random places on its forehead and chest, but they don't amount to much at all.

I hear my wife scream, more like a keening screech, long and loud. As the door closes behind me, I arch my neck over the heads of the women to see my wife one last time, legs pulled wide apart and up, her face red and clenched in pain. The owl sits on the windowsill, looking at her intently. Strong arms grab me. They pull and push me away from the bed, through the door, and out into the hallway.

The door closes firmly.

I press my ear to the door; all is silence beyond.

I try the handle. Locked.

One more thing: the last glimpse I had of my wife was of her lower half, the inside of her thighs. The shoulders of the women in the room had parted briefly, and I saw my baby being born. Just the head was exposed at this early stage.

That's all I saw.

I didn't imagine my baby would be so smooth, round, and white.

THE GHOSTS IN YOU

listen to me because
>I will say this only once
>listen carefully

from the moment of birth
>your many ghosts
>brighten your eyes

sparkle the world
>dance and sing
>play and explore

but ghosts impatient
>catch rides across the
>green earth vanish like

sky color as night rises
>and older now
>a life well-lived

a single piece
>	your ghosts dispersed
>	and your final light

rests reluctant and pale
>	enough to dent a pillow
>	but no more

when at last it finds the courage to
>	leave your body
>	to see if there is anything next

you wish this ghost well as you
>	godspeed the others
>	you remain inanimate

yet wise to the murmur of the
>	unfamiliar the others those strange
>	many who have touched you

the ghosts of
>	everyone you've ever loved
>	that after you've gone

explode into the world
>	only once I will say this
>	listen carefully